U0088086

抓住

文法句型

翻譯寫作

就通了

國家圖書館出版品預行編目資料

抓住文法句型，翻譯寫作就通了 / 何維綺著
-- 初版 -- 新北市：雅典文化，民108.07
面；　公分. --（行動學習；13）
ISBN 978-986-97795-0-0(48K平裝)

1. 英語　2. 語法　3. 句法

805.16　　　　　　　　　　　108007445

行動學習系列　13

抓住文法句型，翻譯寫作就通了

著／何維綺
責任編輯／何維綺
內文排版／王國卿
封面設計／林鈺恆

法律顧問：方圓法律事務所／涂成樞律師

總經銷：永續圖書有限公司　　CVS代理／美璟文化有限公司
永續圖書線上購物網　　　　　TEL：（02）2723-9968
www.foreverbooks.com.tw　　FAX：（02）2723-9668

出版日／2019年07月

雅典文化

出版社
22103　新北市汐止區大同路三段194號9樓之1
TEL　（02）8647-3663
FAX　（02）8647-3660

前言

　　本書之編寫旨在針對英文中常見之文法句型做一簡明及重點式的介紹，不管是在校的學生們，抑或是職場上的社會人士，熟讀本書不僅可對重要的文法句型快速入門，如能對每一個文法句型所附上的文法及翻譯練習題加以實際的演練，對於翻譯及寫作將有紮實的幫助，同時也有助於對英文文章大架構及文意瞭解之增進。

　　而在聽說方面，除了累積單字，其實聽得懂句型，以及說話時能夠用句型表達出來，對於表達能力是很有幫助的。很多人以為聽說只要會大量單字就可以溝通了，當然加上肢體語言這是有可能的，但是如果溝通時沒有以句型架構為基礎，溝通起來是比較費力的，也會花費更多時間，卻不一定達到真正雙方都可以理解的狀態。因此熟讀本書的句型，加上口語運用練習，必然可以增進聽說能力。

　　對於教學上而言，本書也可以是教師們備課時的靈感小幫手，無論是課內的教科書、課外補充教材、學生的作文、或是娛樂性質較高的英文歌曲賞析都可搭配此手冊使用，將其中相關的重點文法用較系統性的手法呈現。

【本書每一個關鍵句型皆有附上文法及翻譯練習題】

三、認識常見的實用句型

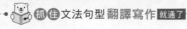

四、認識特殊句型的使用

五、認識常見動詞（片語）的用法

六、認識常見介系詞片語的用法

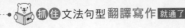
一、認識英文句子的結構

(一) 對等連接詞：

　　主要有and, or, but, so。可將兩個單句連接起來，使其變成複句。

關鍵句型 1：句 + (,) 對等連接詞(and/or/but/so) + 句.

例 The young couple sang and (the young couple) danced all night.
那對年輕夫婦通宵唱歌跳舞。

例 Get up earlier, or you'll be late.
早點起床，否則你會遲到。

例 It is hot in summer in Kaohsiung, but it is not cold in winter.
高雄夏天熱，但冬天不冷。

例 He was sick, so he didn't go to school yesterday.
他生病了，所以昨天沒有上學。

【注意】

★以上四個為最常見的對等連接詞，其他偶爾
會看到的還有：

1. 句, **for** ＋句.
→[for 為對等連接詞，表原因]

例 You should stop smoking, for it is not good
for your health.
你應該要戒菸，因為那對你的健康無益。

2. 句, **yet/while/whereas** ＋句.
→[yet/while/whereas 為對等連接詞，表
「然而，但是」]

例 She didn't know me, yet she helped me.

=She didn't know me, while she helped
me.

=She didn't know me, whereas she
helped me.
她不認識我，但是卻幫了我。

文法練習題

1. He went to Hong Kong in 1980 _____
(he) has lived there ever since.

(A) and

(B) or

(C) ，

(D) X

2. She was exhausted _____ she didn't go to the party last night.
   (A) but
   (B) so
   (C) ，
   (D) X

解答： 1. A 2. B

翻譯練習題

1. 你想要在家裡吃晚餐或是出去吃？
2. 他很生氣，但還是聽了老婆的話。

解答：

1. Would you like to eat dinner at home or (would you like to) dine out?
2. He was very angry, but he still listened to his wife.

關鍵句型 2：如果第一個句子已經很長了，這時可以選擇以下句型來呈現兩個句子：句. 對等連接詞(And/Or/But/So) + 句.

例 Many foreign students think that it is very hard to learn to speak Chinese. But if they keep practicing speaking Chinese, they can become fluent little by little.

許多外國學生認為學習說中文很難。但是只要經常練習，就可以漸漸變得流利。

例 He failed the exam, lost his wallet, and had a fight with his girlfriend yesterday. So don't bother him anymore.

昨天他沒通過考試，丟了錢包，又跟女朋友吵架。所以不要再煩他了。

文法練習題

1. When he was a senior high school student, he did not like to go to school because his teachers gave tests every day. _____ he hated tests.

   (A) Or
   (B) So
   (C) And
   (D) Instead

2. His father had been out of work for two years, and his mother had been in hospital for two months. _____ it was hard for him to make ends meet.

   (A) But
   (B) Luckily
   (C) So
   (D) Instead

解答： 1. C   2. C

翻譯練習題

1. 考試可以激勵學生用功,也可以增進閱讀能力。但是考試太多對他們的健康有害。

2. 派對要到晚上八點才開始,所以我們可以晚點出發。還是你想現在動身?

解答:

1. Tests can stimulate students to hard work, and enhance reading ability. But too many tests are harmful to their health.

2. The party won't take place until 8 p.m., so we can set off later. Or do you want to leave now?

(二) 三大子句:名詞子句、形容詞子句、副詞子句

關鍵句型 1:名詞子句→功用是作為:S或O或C

(1) that + 完整句

例 That he stole your book is a truth.
他偷了你的書是事實。

→紅色部分為 that + 完整句,作為主詞(S)

例 I dozed off and didn't realize that I had missed an important discussion.
我打瞌睡,不知道自己已經錯過了一個重要的討論。

→紅色部分為 that + 完整句，作為受詞
（O）

例 The fact is that the salesperson is dishonest.
事實是這個業務員不老實。

→紅色部分為 that + 完整句，作為補語
（C）

【注意】that + 完整句，也可以作為同位語。

	N	
the/a/an +	fact	+ that + 完整句
	idea	
	conception	
	miralce	
	revelation	

例 You should wake up to the fact that it's a tough world.
你應該領悟到這是個殘酷的世界。

→紅色部分為 that＋完整句，作為 the fact 的同位語。

例 This film was based on the idea that all people have the right of freedom of speech.
這部電影是基於人人皆有言論自由。

→紅色部分為 that＋完整句，作為 the idea 的同位語。

例 The idea that there is really no predictability in nature **has led to the conception** that the universe must be fundamentally chaotic.

自然是不可測的這個想法引導出宇宙基本上是混亂的這個見解。

→紅色部分為 that + 完整句，作為 the idea 和 the conception 的同位語。

例 It is a miracle that she could escape from the kidnapper's place without a scratch.

她能從綁匪之處安然逃脫，真是奇蹟。

→紅色部分為 that + 完整句，作為 a miracle 的同位語。

例 She broke up with him after the revelation that he was addicted to gambling.

在發現他沉迷賭博後，她跟他分手了。

→紅色部分為 that + 完整句，作為 the revelation 的同位語。

【注意】兩個或多個 **that** 所引導的名詞子句當同一 **vt.** 的受詞時，只有第一個 **that** 可以省略，其他不可省略。

例 The thief said (vt.) (that) he was sorry, and that (不可省) he couldn't find a job for a long time.

這個小偷說他很抱歉，很長一段時間他找不到工作。

【補充說明】完整句的定義：[不缺S或O]

1. S + Vt. + O.
   例 I like your watch.
   我喜歡你的錶。

2. S + Vi. (+ 介 + O.)
   例 He often lies, so I don't like to talk to him.
   他常常說謊，所以我不喜歡跟他說話。

3. S + be + pp
   例 He was blamed for his laziness by his parents.
   他的父母親因為他的懶惰而責備他。

   (2) whether + 完整句

★引導名詞子句時or not可放句尾或省略

例 I doubt whether she likes me (or not).
我懷疑她是否喜歡我。

   (3) where/when/how/why + 完整句
   what/who(m) + 不完整句 [缺S或O或C]

例 We don't know | where the superstar lives.
　　　　　　　　| when the old man died.
　　　　　　　　| how the dog got lost.
　　　　　　　　| why the teacher was so angry.
　　　　　　　　| what the little girl is looking for.
　　　　　　　　| who(m) the boy is talking with.

我們不知道那個巨星住在哪裡。
我們不知道那個老先生何時過世。
我們不知道那隻狗怎麼迷失的。
我們不知道老師為何那麼生氣。
我們不知道這個小女孩在找什麼。
我們不知道這個男孩在跟誰說話。

文法練習題

1. We don't know _____ the thief has the
   face to ask for such a thing.
   (A) what
   (B) which
   (C) who
   (D) how

2. He was sleeping then, so he didn't realize
   _____ was going on.
   (A) what
   (B) which
   (C) that
   (D) how

解答： 1. D 2. A

翻譯練習題

1. 麗莎很容易隨心所欲而不顧及他人感受。
2. 你絕對不會體會到你的父母在 1940 年代
   時生活的狀態。

解答：

1. Lisa tends to do what she wants to do without considering people's feelings.
2. You would never know what your parents' life would be like in the 1940s.

關鍵句型 2：形容詞子句

→功用：放在一個名詞後面，來修飾這個
　名詞

→出現的時機很容易判斷，如下：N＋形
　容詞子句

→必須由關係代名詞(which/who/whom/
　whose/that)，所引導出

→關係代名詞的檢查法：

(1) 前面有前置詞(N)。關代就是來取代這
　　個前
　　置詞。

(2) 關代取代後，此關代在其引導的子句
　　中當 S 或 O。

【公式一】 N ＋《關代 ＋ 不完整句》

例 The parrot likes to imitate sounds which it
　heard.

那隻鸚鵡喜歡模仿聽到的聲音。

　→N (sounds) ＋ 關代(which) ＋ 不完整句
　　(it heard) (缺受詞)

　→which 在其後子句中當 O，引導形容詞
　　子句(which it heard)，來修飾 sounds。

例 They were the first men who joined in the singing contest.

他們是最先參加這個唱歌比賽的人。

→N (men) + 關代(who) + 不完整句(joined in the singing contest)(缺主詞)

→who 在其後子句中當 S，引導形容詞子句(who joined in the singing contest)，來修飾 the first men

【公式二】 N +《whose + N + 不完整句》

例 The student comes from an old town whose history goes back to thousands of years.

這個學生來自一個歷史可追溯到幾千年前的古鎮。

→N (town) + whose + N (history) + 不完整句(goes back to thousands of years) (缺主詞)

→whose history 在其後子句中當 S，引導形容詞子句(whose history goes back to thousands of years)，來修飾 town

【公式三】 N +《介 + 關代 + 完整句》

→此時的 介 + 關代 = 關係副詞 (下面的章節會詳細介紹)

例 The ground on which the main actor was standing began to crack.

那個男主角所站立的地面開始破裂。

→N (ground) + 介(on) + 關代(which) + 完整句(the main actor was standing)

→形容詞子句為(on which the main actor was standing)，修飾前置詞 ground (N)

文法練習題

1. The tall building, _____ the Lins lived in, fell down during the earthquake.
   - (A) which
   - (B) in that
   - (C) where
   - (D) whose

2. His parents try to reduce the impact _____ television violence will have on him.
   - (A) where
   - (B) whose
   - (C) who
   - (D) that

解答： **1. A**　　**2. D**

翻譯練習題

1. 約翰看到他所尊敬的那位老師。〔用關係代名詞whom〕
2. 台北是維琪出生的城市。〔用關係代名詞which〕

解答：

1. John saw the teacher whom he respects.
2. Taipei is the city which is Vicky's birthplace.

【公式四】 關係代名詞的省略 (第一種)

→關係代名詞當其引導的形容詞子句的主詞時，就可進行省略

★省略三步驟：

(1) 去掉關係代名詞

(2) 其後動詞改成 V-ing (現在分詞)

(3) 如這個 V-ing (現在分詞)，為 being，則要去掉

例 There are plenty of songs which are written in Taiwanese for us to sing.
有許多用台語寫的歌可供我們歌唱。

→省略三步驟：

第一步去掉 which；第二步 are 改成 being；第三步去掉 being

→所以經過省略之後的句子為 There are plenty of songs written in Taiwanese for us to sing.

例 The man who wears a hat is her boyfriend.
那個戴著帽子的男人是她的男友。

→省略三步驟：

第一步去掉 who；第二步 wears 改成

wearing

→所以經過省略之後的句子為 The man wearing a hat is her boyfriend.

文法練習題

1. I didn't hear anything about the accident _____ in their community yesterday.
   - (A) happened
   - (B) happening
   - (C) which was happened
   - (D) which happening

2. We can see a messy bed _____ with dirty clothes.
   - (A) covering
   - (B) whose covering
   - (C) which covered
   - (D) covered

解答： 1. B　　2. D

翻譯練習題

1. 新搬來我們公寓的住客是個很害羞的人。
2. 夜晚橫越星空看見的銀河是如此美麗。

解答：

1. The resident newly moving to our apartment is a very shy person.
2. The Milky Way seen across the sky at

night is so beautiful.

【公式四】 關係代名詞的省略 (第二種)

→關係代名詞當其引導的形容詞子句的受詞時,「前面沒有逗點或介系詞」,就可以直接省略。

例 I will never forget the lady (whom) I met yesterday.

我絕對不會忘記昨天遇到的那個女士。

→關代在其引導的形容詞子句(whom) I met yesterday 中,作為動詞 met 的受詞,所以可以直接省略。

文法練習題

1. The window _____ you are sitting by is broken.
   - (A) X
   - (B) whose
   - (C) where
   - (D) whom

2. Where is the gift box _____ I received last week?
   - (A) whose
   - (B) who
   - (C) X
   - (D) whom

解答: 1. A 2. C

翻譯練習題

1. 瑪麗正在尋找的那個運動員昨晚上台北了。
2. 我找不到上個月買的那本小說。

解答：

1. The sportsman Mary is looking for went to Taipei last night.
2. I can't find the novel I bought last month.

【公式五】 由關係副詞引導的形容詞子句

→關係副詞＝介系詞＋which（關係代名詞）

→關係副詞＋完整句＝形容詞子句

→關係副詞有四個：where, when, how, why

地方名詞 ＋ **where** ｜＋ 完整句 (不缺主詞或受詞)
時間名詞 ＋ **when** ｜
方法名詞 ＋ **how** ｜
理由名詞 ＋ **why** ｜

例 This is the apartment where I live.
這是我住的公寓。

→地方名詞(the apartment)＋where＋完整句 (I live)

例 There was a period when I was unwilling to talk to him.
有一段時期我不願意跟他說話。

→時間名詞(a period) + when + 完整句
　(I was unwilling to talk to him)

例 That is the way how I practice the guitar.
　那是我練習吉他的方法。

→方法名詞(the way) + how + 完整句
　(I practice the guitar)

→也可以單用 the way 或 how，而寫成：
　That is the way I practice the guitar. 或
　That how I practice the guitar.

例 This is the reason why she cannot see you.
　這就是她無法見你的理由。

→理由名詞(the reason) + why + 完整句
　(she cannot see you)

★補充說明：為何要用關係副詞？
在某些情況下，介詞要用哪一個根本無法決定。

例 Do you know the bank _____ which he caught the robber?

→空格要填介詞，除非你是目擊者，不然搶劫犯如果是在銀行裡被抓到，就要寫成 in which。如果是在銀行附近被抓到，就要寫成 near which。如果是在銀行周圍被抓到，就要寫成 around which。

→介詞到底要用 in，或 near，還是 around，難以決定。

→所以這時用關係副詞，就可以避免這個麻煩了。改寫後的句子為：

例 Do you know the bank where he caught the robber?
你知道他抓到那個搶劫犯的銀行嗎？

★補充說明：關係代名詞與關係副詞之比較，如下所示

N + 《關係代名詞 + 不完整句》

N + 《介 + 關代 + 完整句》

N + 《關係副詞 + 完整句》

文法練習題

1. Being caught in a traffic jam is the reason _____I was late for the meeting.

(A) why

(B) where

(C) how

(D) which

2. Sunday is the day _____ he dines out with his parents.

1. in which

2. when

3. why

4. how

解答： 1. A   2. B

翻譯練習題

1. 我知道一個你們可以一起練習吉他的地方。
2. 我已經改變了我教英文歌的方法。

解答：

1. I know a place where you can practice the guitar together.
2. I've changed the way how I teach English songs.

關鍵句型 3：副詞子句

→副詞連接詞 + 句 = 副詞子句

★ 副詞連接詞的種類

1. 表條件：if, unless (除非), once (一旦), so/as long as (只要)
2. 表時間：when (當) (其後多加非進行式的句子)
   while (正當) (其後多加進行式的句子)
   before/after (在…之前／在…之後)
   until (直到)
   since (自從)
   as soon as (一…就…)
   by the time (到了…之時)
3. 表原因
   because/since/as (因為)
   since/now that (既然)
   although, though (雖然)

4. 表目的

so that = in order that

5. 疑問詞ever = no matter + 疑問詞

★副詞連接詞出現的位置：

1. 句 + 副詞連接詞 + 句.

→紅色字部分為副詞子句

例 My younger brother often disturbs me when I am studying.

我弟弟常常在我唸書時吵我。

例 He didn't turn on the computer until he finished his homework.

一直到他完成了家課，他才打開電腦。

例 You must have more contact with your boyfriend so that you can understand him better.

妳一定要多跟妳的男友接觸，這樣妳才可以更了解他。

2. 副詞連接詞 + 句, 句.

→紅色字部分為副詞子句

例 As soon as the teacher came, the noisy student ran away.

這個老師一來，那個吵鬧的學生拔腿就跑。

例 Before the concert ended, a large rat suddenly fell from the ceiling.

在音樂會結束之前，一隻很大的老鼠突然從天花板掉落。

例 No matter how hard she tries, she never seems to lose any weight.
= However hard she tries, she never seems to lose any weight.
不管她多麼努力嘗試，體重似乎完全沒減輕。

【注意】在副詞子句裡，要用現在式代替未來式。在名詞子句中，則不用代替，該用未來時態時，就用未來式。

1. 在副詞子句裡，用現在式代替未來式

例 If it rains tomorrow, we will stay at home.
如明天下雨，我們將留在家裡。

→[if 子句為副詞子句，故時間雖然是明天，但仍用現在式 rains]

例 When your friend comes to my place, I shall tell him the truth.
當你朋友到我家時，我將告訴他事實。

→[when 子句為副詞子句，故雖然是未來才會發生的事情，但仍用現在式 comes]

2. 在名詞子句裡，該用未來時態，就用未來式。

例 Do you know when your friend will come to our party next time?
你知道你朋友下次何時會來我們的派對嗎？

→[when 子句為名詞子句，作為及物動詞

know 的受詞，從 next time 可知是未來才會發生的事情，故用未來式 will come]

例 Do you know if she <u>will go</u> to the movies with me tomorrow?
你知道她明天會跟我去看電影嗎？
→[if 子句為名詞子句，作為及物動詞 know 的受詞，從 tomorrow 可知是未來才會發生的事情，故用未來式 will go]

【注意】疑問詞-ever = no matter + 疑問詞　不論…

whoever = no matter who 不論是誰
whatever = no matter what 不論什麼
whichever = no matter which 不論哪一個

→**Whoever/Whatever/Whichever**
　(+ 名詞) + 不完整句, 完整句.
= 完整句, **whoever/whatever/whichever**
　(+ 名詞) + 不完整句.

wherever = no matter where 不論在哪裡
whenever = no matter when 不論何時
however = no matter how 不論如何

→**Wherever/Whenever/However** + 完整
　句, 完整句.
= 完整句, **wherever/whenever/however** +
　完整句.

例 You've got a letter from someone called Mary, <u>whoever</u> she may be.
一個名叫瑪麗的人給你一封信，但不清楚她究竟是甚麼人。

例 <u>Whatever</u> he does, his wife doesn't believe him.
不論他做什麼，他的太太都不相信他。

例 <u>Whichever</u> side wins, we will hold a party to celebrate.
不管哪邊贏，我們都會舉行派對來慶祝。

例 <u>Wherever</u> I travel, I make new friends.
不管我到哪裡旅行，我都會結交新朋友。

例 <u>Whenever</u> I think about stray dogs, I feel sad.
每當我想到流浪狗，我就覺得難過。

例 <u>However</u> hot it is, she will not open the air conditioner.
無論多熱，她也不會開冷氣。

文法練習題

1. When I _____ meet Miss Ho tonight, I _____ remind her of the appointment.
   (A) will, will
   (B) X , will
   (C) will, X
   (D) X, X

2. The secretary doesn't know if her boss _____ this evening, but if he _____ , she will tell him the message.
   (A) will come, comes
   (B) comes , will come
   (C) will come, will come
   (D) comes, comes

3. _____ they planned to open a shop in Taipei, they took many goods with them.
   (A) Although
   (B) Because
   (C) If
   (D) Unless

4. Your wife won't forgive you _____ you tell her the truth.
   (A) or
   (B) if
   (C) unless
   (D) when

解答： 1. B 2. A 3. B 4. C

翻譯練習題

1. 門一打開，這隻狗就跑了出去。
2. 到我們再度見面時，你將離開台北。
3. 我們不可再停留，既然計程車在等我們。
4. 只要你用功，你就會通過考試。

解答：

1. As soon as the door was opened, the dog ran out.
2. By the time we meet again, you will have left Taipei.
3. We must not stay any longer now that the taxi is here for us.
   = We must not stay any longer since the taxi is here for us.
4. As long as you study hard, you will pass the exam.

關鍵句型 4：副詞轉折詞

　句; 副詞轉折詞 + 句.

　句. 副詞轉折詞 + 句.

★副詞轉折詞的種類

1. 因此：as a result = therefore = for this reason
   = consequently = hence = accordingly
2. 然而：however = nevertheless =

nonetheless

3. 此外：in addition = moreover = furthermore
   = what's more = besides

例 She caught a serious cold; therefore, she couldn't go with you.

= She caught a serious cold. Therefore, she couldn't go with you.
  她患了重感冒，因此沒辦法跟你一起去。

例 I was very tired; however, I kept on reading the book.

= I was very tired. However, I kept on reading the book.
  我很疲倦，但仍繼續閱讀這本書。

例 Jogging is a good exercise; moreover, it will help you make new friends.

= Jogging is a good exercise.

Moreover, it will help you make new friends.
  慢跑是很好的運動，而且有助於你結交新朋友。

文法練習題

1. The child was down with the flu; _____ _, he couldn't go to school.

   (A) so that

   (B) because

   (C) nevertheless

(D) hence

2. I'm not interested in the party. _____, I have a paper due on Friday, so I won't go to the party with my boyfriend.

(A) Since

(B) However

(C) As a result

(D) Besides

解答： 1. D　　2. D

翻譯練習題

1. 我昨晚熬夜，因此今天早上沒辦法專心聽老師講課。(用 consequently 作答)

2. 去取悅每個人是不可能的，此外我們應該重視自己的想法和主張。(用 in addition 作答)

解答：

1. I stayed up late last night. Consequently, I couldn't pay attention to the teacher this morning. (＝ I stayed up late last night; consequently, I couldn't pay attention to the teacher this morning.)

2. It is impossible to please everybody. In addition, we should value our own thoughts and ideas. (＝ It is impossible to please everybody; in addition, we should value our own thoughts and ideas.)

二、認識重要時態的運用

關鍵句型 1：在做⋯時

★ **in + V-ing = when + V-ing** 在做...時

例 He should watch the traffic light <u>in crossing</u> the street.

= He should watch the traffic light <u>when crossing</u> the street.

他在過馬路的時候，應該要注意紅綠燈。

例 <u>In raising</u> money to support his work, John made contact with many big companies.

= <u>When raising</u> money to support his work, John made contact with many big companies.

約翰在籌款以支持他的工作時，接觸過許多大公司。

文法練習題

1. _____ the machine, you should follow the directions.

(A) In operation

(B) In operating

(C) when you operating

(D) You operate

2. Be sure to make eye contact with your boss _____ talking to him.

(A) when you

(B) you

(C) when

(D) you are

解答: **1. B**　　**2. C**

翻譯練習題

1. 在練習鋼琴時，她很仔細聽。

2. 在寫英文作文時，他總是覺得不安。

解答:

1. She listened closely in/when practicing the piano.

(=In/When practicing the piano, She listened closely.)

2. He always feels upset in/when writing an English composition.

= In/When writing an English composition, he always feels upset.

關鍵句型 2: 一…就…

★ **On/Upon** + V-ing, 句.　一…就…

= S + **had** + **no sooner** + pp + **than** + 句 (過去式).

= S + **had** + **hardly** + pp + **when** + 句 (過去式).

= **As soon as** + 句 (過去式), 句 (過去
式).

【提醒】用 **had** + **pp** 的句型，是強調先發生
的動作，雖然這個動作發生的時間
也早不了多少。

例 The naughty student ran away on/upon
seeing the military instructor.

= The military instructor had no sooner come
than the naughty student ran away.

= The military instructor had hardly come
when the naughty student ran away.

= As soon as the military instructor came, the
naughty student ran away.
教官一來，那個頑皮的學生拔腿就跑。

例 He rushed to the scene on/upon hearing "
about the car accident.

= He had no sooner heard about the car
accident than he rushed to the scene.

= He had hardly heard about the car accident
when he rushed to the scene.

= He rushed to the scene as soon as he heard
about the car accident.
他一聽到車禍就趕到現場。

文法練習題

1. As soon as the couple reached the seaside, they _____ the magnificent sea.
   - (A) were attracted by
   - (B) were attracting
   - (C) had been attracted by
   - (D) had attracted

2. I had _____ in when I told the driver where I was going.
   - (A) no sooner got
   - (B) getting
   - (C) hardly got
   - (D) as soon as got

解答： **1. A**　**2. C**

翻譯練習題

1. 一聽到新聞，凱麗就突然哭了起來。
   【用 On + V-ing...】
2. 男主角一上台，觀眾就大喊大叫。【用 As soon as...】

解答：

1. On hearing the news, Kelly burst into tears.
2. As soon as the leading actor came on stage, the audience shouted and screamed.

關鍵句型 3：經過…時間

★ **over/in/during** + **the** + **past/last** + 一段時間

經過…時間 [用現在完成式]

例 The consumer market in Taiwan <u>has changed</u> quite a lot over the past ten years.
台灣的消費市場最近十年變了很多。

例 During the last two years, I <u>have learned</u> a lot of things in the community university.
過去兩年來，我在社區大學學到了不少東西。

文法練習題

1. Over the last twenty years, the actress _____ two Grammy Awards.
   (A) wins
   (B) won
   (C) was winning
   (D) has won

2. I love dogs so much that I _____ three dogs for the past ten years.
   (A) keep
   (B) am keeping
   (C) kept
   (D) have kept

解答： **1. D**　　**2. D**

翻譯練習題

1. 最近兩年他寫了兩本書。【用 In the past...】

2. 近十年來,嘉義的街景有了相當大的改變。
   【用 Over the past...】

解答:

1. In the past two years, he has written two books.

2. Over the past ten years, the street scenes of Chia-yi have changed considerably.

關鍵句型 4:該是…的時候了

★ **it is time + (that) 句【that 子句裡用過去式動詞】**

= **it is time + for 人 + to V**

該是…的時候了 (跟現在事實相反)

例 It is time (that) we <u>went</u> to the train station.

= It is time for us to go to the train station.
  該是我們去車站的時候了。

例 The clock struck eleven. It was time (that) I <u>went</u> to bed.

= The clock struck eleven. It was time for me to goto bed.
  時鐘敲了十一下。我該上床睡覺了。

文法練習題

1. It's time you _____ to her about your debt.
   - (A) talk
   - (B) talked
   - (C) will talk
   - (D) talking

2. It's time that you _____ back.
   - (A) fighting
   - (B) should have fought
   - (C) fight
   - (D) fought

解答： **1. B**　　**2. D**

翻譯練習題

1. 該是你面對現實的時候了。
2. 該是你先生承擔責任的時候了。

解答：

1. It's time (that) you faced the music.
   (= It's time for you to face the music.)
2. It's time that your husband accepted responsibility.
   (= It's time for your husband to accept responsibility.)

關鍵句型 5：by the time

【公式一】

by the time [= 副詞連接詞] 在…之前
(另一個動作早已發生了)

句 (過去完成式) + 《**by the time** + 句
(過去式).》

句 (未來完成式) + 《**by the time** + 句
(現在式).》

例 By the time I <u>arrived</u> at the bus stop, the
bus <u>had left</u>.
在我抵達公車站之前，公車已經開走了。

例 Miss Chen <u>will have taught</u> here for three
years by the time you <u>come</u> here next year.
你明年來到這裡之前，陳老師將任教滿三
年。

【公式二】

by the time [= 副詞連接詞] 到…時

句 (過去式) + 《**by the time** + 句 (過
去式).》

句 (未來式) + 《**by the time** + 句 (現
在式).》

例 By the time they <u>arrived</u> at the office, they
<u>were</u> pretty worn out.
當他們到達辦公室時，他們精疲力盡。

例 By the time you <u>receive</u> his letter, he <u>will be</u> in Hong Kong.
當你收到他的信時,他人將在香港。

文法練習題

1. I hope that by the time you are ready to go to college, you will _____ a better idea of what you want to do.
   (A) be
   (B) be having
   (C) had had
   (D) have had

2. By the time she started to learn Japanese, she _____ five languages.
   (A) has already learned
   (B) had already learned
   (C) already learned
   (D) was learning

解答: 　　1. D　　2. B

翻譯練習題

1. 到了我醒來的時候,我累得走不動。
2. 在他出生前,他的父母已經幫他買了很多書。

解答：

1. By the time I woke up, I was too tired to walk.

2. By the time he was born, his parents had bought many books for him.

關鍵句型 6：since的用法

【公式一】

句 (現在完成式／現在完成進行式) +
《since (自從) + 時間片語／時間副詞／
句 (過去式).》

→用 ever since 也可以，跟 since 的差別
在於語氣較強烈。

例 I haven't heard from Mr. Wang since two years ago.
自從兩年前以來我未曾有過王老師的消息。

例 Since then, I have realized that I have to be independent.
自從那時起，我就瞭解到我必須獨立。

例 She has become much more sure of herself since she joined the singing club.
自從她加入那個歌唱社後，她變得有自信多了。

例 He has been living a hard life since his wife died.

自從老婆死後，他一直過著孤獨的生活。

【公式二】

句 (過去完成式／過去完成進行式) +
《since (自從) + 時間片語／時間副詞／
句 (過去式).》

→過去某段時間內的持續，未延續到現
在，故主要子句用「過去完成式」或
「過去完成進行式」。

例 The school had completely changed since
I went there five years ago.
自從我五年前去過那個學校以後，已經完
全變樣了。

例 Since I left, they had been fighting for two
years.
自從我離開後，他們持續吵架了兩年之
久。

文法練習題

1. Since then, Vicky _____ that nothing
   is certain.
   (A) realizes
   (B) realized
   (C) has realized
   (D) had been realized

2. Ever since we met last time, our friendship
   _____.

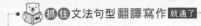

(A) has strengthened

(B) strengthened

(C) has been strengthened

(D) strengthens

解答： 1. C 2. C

翻譯練習題

1. 自從那次車禍後，我就下定決心要助人。
2. 我們結婚到現在已經三年了。

解答：

1. Ever since the car accident, I have made up my mind to help people.
2. It has been three years since we married.

關鍵句型 7：for的用法：

句 (現在完成式／現在完成進行式) + for 一段時間

【注意】此種用法中的動詞不可為瞬間動詞 (瞬間動詞：無法延續的動詞，動作一發生狀態就改變，如die, marry)。

例 I have lived in Taipei for five years.
我住在台北已有五年。

例 It has been raining for three days.
已經連續下三天的雨了。（說話的同時雨還在下著）

例 The old man has been dead for a week.
(= The old man died a week ago.)
老先生已過世一個禮拜了。

[不可用 The old man has died for a week.
因為 die 是瞬間動詞，動作一發生狀態
就改變，無法延續]

文法練習題

1. _____ many years, Dr. Ho has devoted
his time to discovering the secrets of how
the mind does its work.
  (A) For
  (B) Before
  (C) After
  (D) Of

2. Mr. Chen _____ for more than ten years.
  (A) married
  (B) was married
  (C) has married
  (D) has been married

解答： 1. A   2. D

翻譯練習題

1. 我已經在這等你三十分鐘了。
2. 我很久以前就在想我的生涯規劃。

解答：

1. I have been waiting for you here for more than thirty minutes.
2. I've been thinking for a long time about my career planning.

關鍵句型 8：wish的用法

★ S + wish + (that) 假設句.

→假設句裡：

were 過去式動詞 過去式助動詞 + V	與現在事實相反
had + pp	與過去事實相反

例 I wish (that) I were in the office now.
[與現在事實相反]

真希望我現在人在辦公室。

→但事實上，我人現在不在辦公室。

例 He wishes (that) he had met me at the dancing party yesterday.
[與過去事實相反]

他很希望昨晚在舞會上與我相遇。

→但事實上，昨晚他並沒有遇到我。

文法練習題

1. My husband wishes he _____ go to work today.
   - (A) X
   - (B) has to
   - (C) didn't have to
   - (D) doesn't have to

2. I wish she _____ behind my back in the presence of my boss in the meeting yesterday.
   - (A) talked
   - (B) had talked
   - (C) didn't talk
   - (D) hadn't talked

解答： 1. C　　2. D

翻譯練習題

1. 我希望我的父親會發覺我的天賦而給我更多的自由。
2. 她先生希望有一百萬，那他就可以買新車。

解答：

1. I wish (that) my father would discover my talent and give me more freedom.
2. Her husband wishes (that) he had one million dollars so that he could buy a new car.

關鍵句型 9：假設語氣

【重點一】與現在事實相反的假設語氣

If + 主詞 + 過去式動詞/were...,	+ 主詞 + 過去式助動詞 (should/would/could/might) + 原形動詞
But for/Without + 名詞 (片語),	

例 If I were you, I would go to the party.
如果我是你，我會去派對。

【In fact, I am not you, and I will not go to the party. 事實上，我不是你，我也不會去派對。→跟現在事實相反】

例 If I had one hundred thousand dollars, I could travel around Taiwan.
如果我有十萬，我可以環遊台灣。

【In fact, I don't have one hundred thousand dollars, and I can't travel around Taiwan. 事實上，我沒有十萬，我也無法環遊台灣。→跟現在事實相反】

例 But for your suggestion, I might go astray.
= Without your suggestion, I might go astray.
如果不是你的建議，我也許會誤入歧途。

【In fact, you give me your suggestion, and I don't go astray. 事實上，你給我你

的建議，而且我沒有誤入歧途。→跟現在
事實相反】

【重點二】與過去事實相反的假設語氣

If + 主詞 + had pp...,	+ 主詞 + 過去式助動詞 (should/would/could/might) + have pp
But for/Without + 名詞(片語),	

例 If my mother had had enough money, she would have bought that coffee machine last night.
如果我媽媽有足夠的錢，昨晚她就會買下那台咖啡機。

【In fact, my mother didn't have enough money, and she didn't buy that coffee machine last night.
事實上，昨晚我媽媽沒有足夠的錢，而且她也沒有買下那台咖啡機。→跟過去事實相反】

例 But for your financial assistance, the restaurant should have been closed down two months ago.
= Without your financial assistance, the restaurant should have been closed down two months ago.

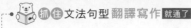

= If it had not been for your financial assistance, the restaurant should have been closed down two months ago.
如果不是因為你的資助,這家餐廳應該兩個月前就要停業了。

【In fact, you offered your financial assistance to the restaurant, so it hadn't been closed down two months ago.
事實上,你資助了這家餐廳,所以兩個月前它沒有停業。→跟過去事實相反】

【重點三】不協調的假設句

If + 句 (had+pp),	句【過去式助動詞(should/would/could/might) + 原形動詞】.
→如果當時… (與過去事實相反)	→現在就… (與現在事實相反)

例 If I had studied hard last year, I should enter an ideal university now.
如果去年我用功讀書,現在應該就會進入理想的大學就讀了。

【In fact, I didn't study hard last year, so I don't enter an ideal university now. 事實上,去年我並沒有用功讀書,所以現在也沒有進入理想的大學就讀。→一邊與過去事實相反,另一邊與現在事實相反,所以是不協調的假設句。】

例 If she had met you yesterday, she would stay in Taipei now.
如果她昨天有遇到你，她現在就會待在台北了。

【In fact, she didn't meet you yesterday, so she is not in Taipei now. 事實上，她昨天並沒有遇見你，所以她人現在也不在台北。→一邊與過去事實相反，另一邊與現在事實相反，所以是不協調的假設句。】

文法練習題

1. If I had earned a lot of money, I _____ a new house last year.
   (A) would buy
   (B) would have bought
   (C) have bought
   (D) will buy

2. If Bill _____ in the presidential place two years ago, his company should make a lot of money now.
   (A) sits
   (B) sat
   (C) had sat
   (D) had been sat

解答：　1. B　　2. C

翻譯練習題

1. 如果我是這位病人,我會多吃蔬果。
   【用 If I...】
2. 如果你兩年前在那家公司工作,你現在
   應該當經理了。【用 If you...】

解答:

1. If I were the patient, I would eat vegetables
   and fruits more.
2. If you had worked in that company two
   years ago, you should be a manager now.

關鍵句型 10:與過去事實相反的獨立句

★與過去事實相反的假設語氣,並非一定要用
在 if 出現的句子裡,一般句子裡只要出現以
下四種結構,即可成為與過去事實相反的獨
立句。

與過去事實相反的結構	
should (= ought to) + have pp	過去該…,但沒…
would + have pp	過去會…,但沒…
could + have pp	過去能…,但沒…
needn't (不必) + have pp	表過去不必…,但做了

例 You should have helped me yesterday.
昨天你應該幫我的。

[與過去事實相反→In fact, you didn't help me yesterday. 事實上，你昨天沒有幫我。]

例 Luckily, you took my advice. Otherwise, I am sure that you would have failed English last semester.

幸運地，你聽了我的建議。不然我敢確定上學期你英文會不及格。

[與過去事實相反→In fact, you didn't fail English last semester because you took my advice. 事實上，上學期你英文及格了，因為你有聽我的建議。]

例 You could have enjoyed the appointment with him. The problem was that he just talked too much.

你跟他約會可以很愉快的。問題出在他話太多。

[與過去事實相反→In fact, you didn't enjoy the appointment with him because he talked too much. 事實上，你跟他的約會並不愉快，因為他話太多。]

例 We still had plenty of time; we needn't have hurried then.

我們還有很多時間，我們那時候並不需要趕時間的。

[與過去事實相反→In fact, we hurried then even though we had plenty of time. 事實上，我們那時候很匆忙，即使我們有很多時間，]

文法練習題

1. I failed in the history exam this morning. I ＿＿ my lessons last night, but I didn't.
   - (A) should have studied
   - (B) might have studied
   - (C) must have studied
   - (D) can have studied

2. My husband ＿＿ that position but for his best friend's help in those days.
   - (A) could earn
   - (B) could not earn
   - (C) could not have earned
   - (D) had not attained

解答： 1. A 2. C

翻譯練習題

1. 你現在做的是早就應該完成的事。
2. 今天我不用去上班，原本我可以睡晚一點的。

解答：

1. You are doing what should have been finished earlier.

2. I don't have to work today and I could have slept late.

關鍵句型 11：as if, as though

★ as if = as though 彷彿【為副詞連接詞】

【重點一】句 + as if／as though + 一般陳述句.

→常和 look, seem, appear 連用。

→It + looks/seems/appears + as if + 句.

例 It seems as if my son has lost interest in his job.

= It appears as though my son has lost interest in his job.

我兒子似乎對自己的工作已失去興趣。

【重點二】句 + as if／as though + 假設句.

→假設句裡，過去 V／were = 與現在事實相反

→假設句裡，had + pp = 與過去事實相反

例 She treats me as if I were a stranger.

她待我如陌生人。

→[But in fact for her I am not a stranger.

但事實上對她來說，我並非陌生人。]

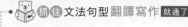

例 The reporter talks as though she <u>had heard</u> about the news yesterday.

那個記者講話的樣子好像昨天她就得知這個消息了。

→[But in fact the reporter didn't hear about the news yesterday.

但事實上那個記者昨天並沒有聽聞這個消息。]

文法練習題

1. The curious boy likes to stare at me as if I ＿＿＿ his favorite cartoon character, Doraemon.

   (A) am
   (B) was
   (C) were
   (D) being

2. He broke my window this morning. But he behaved as if nothing ＿＿＿.

   (A) happens
   (B) happened
   (C) was happening
   (D) had happened

解答： 1. C 　 2. D

翻譯練習題

1. 那輛計程車看起來好像是全新的。
   【用現在式一般陳述句】
2. 他一直打哈欠，好像昨天整個晚上熬夜。
   【用 as if + 假設句】

解答：

1. That taxi looks as if/as though it is brand-new.
2. He keeps yawning as if he had stayed up all night yesterday.

關鍵句型 12：推測語氣

★ must/may/might + 原V [對現在推測]

must/may/might + have pp [對過去推測]

例 My younger sister is a nurse. She may help you.
我妹妹是個護士。她或許可以幫你。

例 He might have said so, though he seems to forget it.
他或許說過那樣的話，雖然他好像忘記了。

文法練習題

1. Bill couldn't find his watch. He must
   ____ it.
   (A) lose
   (B) lost
   (C) have lost
   (D) be losing

2. It _____ last night, for I found the
   flowers in my garden were wet this
   morning.
   (A) rains
   (B) rained
   (C) might rain
   (D) might have rained

解答： **1. C** **2. D**

翻譯練習題

1. 他看起來很生氣。我猜想我一定是有什
   麼地方得罪了他。
2. 我睡不好，我可能有睡眠障礙。

解答：

1. He looks very angry. I suppose I must
   have offended him in some way.
2. I can't sleep well; I may experience
   sleeping difficulties.

關鍵句型 13：兩個動作一短一長

【重點一】在過去，有兩個動作一短一長，短的動作發生在長的動作之內，長者用「過去進行式」，短者用「過去簡單式」。

例 The dog <u>was</u> almost <u>hit</u> by a car while it <u>was crossing</u> the street.

那隻狗在過街時差點被一輛車子給撞了。

→[過街是長動作，所以用過去進行式。被撞是短動作，所以用過去簡單式。]

例 When I <u>met</u> him at the restaurant, he <u>was speaking</u> on the phone.

當我在餐廳遇見他時，他正在講電話。

→[講電話是長動作，所以用過去進行式。遇見他是短動作，所以用過去簡單式。]

【重點二】在未來，有兩個動作一短一長，短的動作發生在長的動作之內，長者用「未來進行式」，短者用「未來簡單式」。

【提醒】要注意副詞子句裡，要用「現在簡單式」代替「未來簡單式」。

例 He will be studying all the morning
　 tomorrow when you come to see him here.
　 明天早上當你來這裡看他時，他將在K書
　 狀態。

→[K書是長動作，所以用未來進行式。來
　看他是短動作，所以用簡單式（用
　come 而不用 will come，因為是在副詞
　子句裡，所以用「現在簡單式」代替
　「未來簡單式」）。]

文法練習題

1. While my girlfriend was traveling in Japan,
　 she _____ an old friend of hers.
　 (A) meets
　 (B) met
　 (C) had met
　 (D) was meeting

2. While I _____, a fly flew into my mouth.
　 (A) yawn
　 (B) yawned
　 (C) was yawning
　 (D) had yawned

解答：　1. B　　2. C

翻譯練習題

1. 今晚當你來到我的書店時，她將正在為最新的小說替讀者簽名。
2. 有一天當這個警察正在做例行的檢查時，那位經理送他一些錢賄賂他。

解答：

1. She will be signing copies of her latest novel when you come to my bookstore tonight.
2. One day while the policeman was doing his routine inspection, the manager bribed him by giving him some money.

關鍵句型 14：兩個動作一先一後

【重點一】在過去，有兩個動作，一個先發生，一個後發生，先發生的用「過去完成式」，後發生的用「過去簡單式」。

例 The discussion began after we had had lunch.
討論在我們用過午餐後開始。
→[用午餐是先發生的動作，所以用過去完成式。討論開始是後發生的動作，所以用過去簡單式]

例 He gave me the book which he had bought last night.
他給我昨晚已經買好的書。

→[買書是先發生的動作，所以用過去完成式。給我書是後發生的動作，所以用過去簡單式]

【重點二】在未來，有兩個動作，一個先發生，一個後發生，先發生的用「未來完成式」，後發生的用「未來簡單式」。

【提醒】要注意副詞子句裡，要用「現在(完成)式」代替「未來(完成)式」。

例 I will take a rest after I have done my work.
我做完工作後會休息一下。

→[做完工作是先發生的動作，所以用完成式。（用 have done 而不用 will have done，因為是在副詞子句裡，所以用「現在完成式」代替「未來完成式」。）]

→[休息一下是後發生的動作，所以用未來簡單式。]

文法練習題

1. Yesterday her students _____ her for what she _____.
   (A) thanked; had done
   (B) thanked; did
   (C) had thanked; had done
   (D) had thanked; did

2. I ＿＿＿ you some money when I have won the lottery.

(A) lend

(B) lent

(C) will lend

(D) will have lent

解答： 1. A 2. C

翻譯練習題

1. 當我抵達火車站的時候，火車已經開走了。

2. 你明年來這裡的時候，何老師將任教滿二年。

解答：

1. When I arrived at the train station, the train had already left.

2. Miss Ho will have taught here for three years when you come here next year.

→[用 come 而不用 will come，因為是在副詞子句裡，所以用「現在簡單式」代替「未來簡單式」。]

三、認識常見的實用句型

關鍵句型 1：因果句型

【重點一】Because 句, 句.

= 句 because 句.

= 句, for 句.

例 At that time, because the teachers gave tests every day, I did not like to go to school.

= At that time, I did not like to go to school because the teachers gave tests every day.

= At that time, I did not like to go to school, for the teachers gave tests every day.
那時候我不喜歡上學，因為老師每天都考試。

例 Because Uncle Sam forgot, he didn't show up for our dancing party.

= Uncle Sam didn't show up for our dancing party because he forgot.

= Uncle Sam didn't show up for our dancing party, for he forgot.
我們的舞會，山姆叔叔沒有來，因為他忘了。

【重點二】原V, and (那麼) + 句.

原V, or (否則) + 句.

例 Study hard, and you will pass the exam.
用功讀書，你會通過考試的。

例 Eat right food and take exercise every day, and you'll be more and more beautiful.
每日吃正確的食物及運動，你會越來越漂亮。

例 Hurry up, or you'll miss the train.
快點，否則你會錯過火車。

例 Get up early, or you'll be late for the meeting.
早點起床，否則你開會會遲到。

【提醒】否定時在V前，加 don't

例 Don't talk back to Mr. Wang, or he'll be very sad.
別跟王老師頂嘴，否則他會很傷心的。

【重點三】如此地…以致於…

★so + adj／adv + that句
★so + adj／adv + as to V

例 The rich man was so superior that no one would like to make friends with him.
那個富人是如此地高傲以致於沒有一個人願意跟他做朋友。

→[可改寫成：The rich man was so superior as to have no friends.
那個富人是如此地高傲以致於沒有朋友。]

例 They sang so loudly that I could hardly sleep.

他們唱得那麼大聲以致於我幾乎無法入睡。

→[可改寫成：They sang so loudly as to make me sleepless.

他們唱得那麼大聲以致於讓我睡不著。]

【重點四】如此的⋯以致於⋯

★ such + 任何形式的名詞 (單複數或不可數名詞) + that 句

→such 為形容詞，之後可接任何形式的名詞

例 such a cute child (單數) 一個如此可愛的孩子

例 such good friends (複數) 這麼好的朋友

例 such dirty money (不可數名詞) 這麼骯髒的錢

例 He is such a strict teacher that some of his students don't like him.

他是一個如此嚴格的老師，以致於有一些他的學生不喜歡他。

例 Iman and Tracy are such nice pets that they have become members of my family. 依馬跟崔西是如此好的寵物，他們已經成為我的家人。

【提醒】such + a + adj + N + that 句 如此一個⋯以致於⋯

= so + adj + a + N + that 句

例 It was such a nice day that we decided to go to the Taipei zoo.

= It was so nice a day that we decided to go to the Taipei zoo.
天氣這麼好，因此我們決定要去台北市立動物園。

【重點五】The + 比較級 + 餘句, the + 比較級 + 餘句.

1. 找出原句中的「adj／adv／N」
2. 改成比較級，搬到句首the之後
   →the + adj 比較級／adv 比較級
   ›the + more/less/fewer + N
3. 加入餘句:
   The + adj/adv/N-比較級 + 餘句, the + adj/adv/N -比較級 + 餘句.

例 You are honest. Your friends will take your words seriously. (原句)
   →The more honest you are, the more seriously your friends will take your words.

   (因果句) 你越誠實，你的朋友就會越重視你所說的話。

例 Your children get advice on how to manage their time.

They are not <u>likely</u> to get into trouble (原句)

→The more advice your children get on how to manage their time, <u>the less likely</u> they are to get into trouble.

你的小孩得到更多管理時間的建議，他們就更能避免不必要的煩惱。

文法練習題

1. Go there by taxi, _____ we will miss the show.
   - (A) or
   - (B) and
   - (C) however
   - (D) otherwise

2. I think my boss looks down on me _____ I am female.
   - (A) because of
   - (B) moreover
   - (C) therefore
   - (D) because

3. When the doctor told her she could go home, she felt _____ happy that she had completely forgotten the pains.
   - (A) such
   - (B) as

(C) so

(D) for

4. The ＿＿ learned a man is, the ＿＿ modest he usually is.

(A) more/more

(B) many/many

(C) much/much

(D) X/X

5. The old man only eats two meals each day. He believes the ＿＿ he eats, the ＿＿ he lives.

(A) more/more

(B) more/little

(C) less/longer

(D) less/much

解答： 1. A 2. D 3. C 4. A 5. C

翻譯練習題

1. 小心應對我們的願望，因為它有可能成真。

2. 持續練習，你就會投進更多球。

3. 一切發生的這麼快，她根本沒有時間思考。

4. 有些人對音樂是如此熱情，他們會整晚不睡覺聽最喜愛的CDs。

5. 你工作越努力，你就越有可能成功。

解答：

1. Be careful about what we wish for because it just might come true.

2. Keep practicing, and you'll make more shots.

3. Everything happened so suddenly that she didn't have any time to think.

4. Some people have such a passion for music that they will stay up all night listening to their favorite CDs.

5. The harder you work, the more likely you are to succeed.

關鍵句型 2：目的句型

[→此句型牽涉到動作的目的，基本概念是：目的是未來的事情。]

【重點一】 **(In order) to + V, 句.**

　　　　　 = 句 + **(in order) to + V.**

　　　　　 = 句 + **so as to + V.**

【重點二】

★句 + **so that** 句【有助動詞】.

　= 句 + **in order that** 句【有助動詞】.

例 (In order) to enter the apartment, the thief broke the window.

= The thief broke the window (in order) to enter the apartment.

= The thief broke the window so as to enter

the apartment.

= The thief broke the window <u>so that</u> he could enter the apartment.

= The thief broke the window <u>in order that</u> he could enter the apartment.

為了進入那棟公寓，那個小偷打破窗戶。

例 <u>(In order) to help</u> stray dogs, she donated some money to the non-profit organization.

= She donated some money to the non-profit organization <u>(in order) to help</u> stray dogs.

= She donated some money to the non-profit organization <u>(so as) to help</u> stray dogs.

= She donated some money to the non-profit organization <u>so that</u> she could help stray dogs.

= She donated some money to the non-profit organization <u>in order that</u> she could help stray dogs.

為了幫助流浪狗，她捐了一些錢給這個非營利組織。

【重點三】

★With a view to + N/V-ing, 句.

[= 句 with a view to + N/V-ing.]

= With an eye to + N/V-ing, 句.

[= 句 with an eye to + N/V-ing.]

= For the purpose of + N/V-ing, 句.

[= 句 for the purpose of + N/V-ing.]

= For the sake of + N/V-ing, 句.

[= 句 for the sake of + N/V-ing.]

例 My daughter studied hard with a view to passing the final exam.

= My daughter studied hard with an eye to passing the final exam.

= My daughter studied hard for the purpose of passing the final exam.

= My daughter studied hard for the sake of passing the final exam.

我女兒努力用功目的是要通過期末考。

例 With a view to helping stray dogs, she donated some money to the non-profit organization.

= With an eye to helping stray dogs, she donated some money to the non-profit organization.

= For the purpose of helping stray dogs, she donated some money to the non-profit organization.

= For the sake of helping stray dogs, she donated some money to the non-profit organization.

為了幫助流浪狗,她捐了一些錢給這個非營利組織。

文法練習題

1. You don't need any special clothes _____ participate in this activity.
   - (A) to
   - (B) so that
   - (C) with
   - (D) in

2. Drink more warm water _____ you can recover soon.
   - (A) in order to
   - (B) so that
   - (C) so as to
   - (D) and this

解答： 1. A   2. B

翻譯練習題

1. 我的經理常常揮動雙手來強調他講的話。
   【用 for the purpose of, 放句中】
2. 我註冊這個課程是為了改善我的英文口說能力。
   【用 to + V, 放句中】

解答：

1. My manager often moves his hands for the purpose of emphasizing what he is saying.
2. I enrolled in this course to improve my English speaking ability.

關鍵句型 3：常見片語, + 句.

【重點一】表「有」跟「沒有」

★ With + N/V-ing, 句. = [句 with + N/V-ing.]	有…
★ Without + N/V-ing, 句. = [句 without + N/V-ing.]	沒有…

例 With money, we can buy many things.
= We can buy many things with money.
　有了錢我們可以買很多東西。

例 With all my faults, my mother still loves me.
= My mother still loves me with all my faults.
　儘管我有許多缺點，我媽媽仍然愛我。

例 Without knocking at the door, the child entered my room.
= The child entered my room without knocking at the door.
　這個小孩沒敲門就進來我房間了。

例 Without a word, my husband left us.
= My husband left us without a word.
　我先生一句話也沒說就離開了我們。

【提醒】with + O + adj／分詞／介片
　　　 表附帶狀態

例 The superstar held a great feast with wine and food enough for the guests.
這個超級巨星舉行大型宴會,豐盛的酒和食物足夠賓客享用。

例 I walked back to my house, with a strange man following me.
我走回我家,後面有一個奇怪的人跟著。

例 My girlfriend had fallen asleep with her head against my shoulder.
我女友已經睡著了,頭還靠在我的肩膀上。

【重點二】就…而言、鑒於…

★ In terms of + N/V-ing, 句.
  = [句 in terms of + N/V-ing.]

★ In the light of + N/V-ing, 句.
  = [句 in the light of + N/V-ing.]

★ In view of + N/V-ing, 句.
  = [句 in view of + N/V-ing.]

例 This school provides students with first-class studying environment. In terms of software, courses and teaching are arranged satisfactorily.

= This school provides students with first-class studying environment. In the light of software, courses and teaching are arranged satisfactorily.

= This school provides students with first-class studying environment. <u>In view of software</u>, courses and teaching are arranged satisfactorily.

這間學校提供學生第一流的學習環境。就教學軟體而言，課程和教學包你滿意。

例 He reviewed his investment strategy <u>in terms of recent developments</u>.

= He reviewed his investment strategy <u>in the light of recent developments</u>.

= He reviewed his investment strategy <u>in view of recent developments</u>.

鑒於最近的事態發展，他重新考慮自己的投資策略。

【重點三】根據⋯

★ **Based on + N/V-ing, 句.**
= **[句 based on + N/V-ing.]**

★ **According to + N/V-ing, 句.**
= **[句 according to + N/V-ing.]**

例 Please put the books on the shelves <u>according to size</u>.

= Please put the books on the shelves <u>based on size</u>.

請按大小將書放到書架上。

例 <u>According to my observation</u>, he often stays up late.

= Based on my observation, he often stays up late.
根據我的觀察，他常常熬夜。

【重點四】說到…

★ Speaking of + N/V-ing, 句.
　= [句 speaking of + N/V-ing.]

★ When it comes to + N/V-ing, 句.
　= [句 when it comes to + N/V-ing.]

例 Speaking of influence, the language you speak matters.

= When it comes to influence, the language you speak matters.
說到影響力，說的語言很重要。

例 Proper exercise is important speaking of taking care of health.

= Proper exercise is important when it comes to taking care of health.
說到照顧健康，適當的運動是重要的。

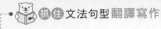

【重點五】**to +人's + 情緒性名詞**

		情緒性名詞	中文意思
to	人's	**surprise**	令某人驚訝的是…
		amazement	令某人驚異的是…
		relief	令某人安心的是…
		disappointment	令某人失望的是…
		delight	令某人喜悅的是…

例 To my surprise, my student refused to talk with me.

令我吃驚的是，我的學生不肯跟我說話。

例 Much to my relief, the stray dog is safe now.

這隻流浪狗現在沒事了，我大大鬆了一口氣。

→[much 是用來加強語氣。]

例 To our great disappointment, the singer did not join in the activity.

使我們大失所望的是，那個歌手沒有參加活動。

→[great 是用來加強程度。]

文法練習題

1. If you are not sure how to answer, make your choice ____ your most typical response in the given situation.
   - (A) as long as
   - (B) without
   - (C) when it comes to
   - (D) based on

2. The artist walked slowly, with her hands ____ behind her back.
   - (A) fold
   - (B) folds
   - (C) folded
   - (D) folding

3. We are prone to interpret the meaning of an incident ____ our own experiences.
   - (A) without
   - (B) in terms of
   - (C) because
   - (D) including

解答： 1. D   2. C   3. B

翻譯練習題

1. 陳老師一直上課，沒有看見她的學生昏昏欲睡。
   〔用 without〕
2. 令瑪莉喜悅的是，這次的小考她得了一百分。
3. 隨著時間的流逝，我逐漸體會他們不可能永遠支持我。〔用 with〕

解答：

1. Miss Chen kept teaching without seeing (that) her students were sleepy.
2. To Mary's delight, she got a score of 100 on the quiz.
3. With time passing by, I came to realize (that) they could not always support me.

關鍵句型 4：too + adj/adv + to V 太…以致於不…

★ too + adj/adv + (for 人) + to V

例 The child is <u>too</u> young <u>to</u> tell right from wrong.
這個小孩年紀太小以致於無法分辨是非。

例 You speak <u>too</u> fast for me <u>to</u> understand.
你說得太快了，我無法理解。

文法練習題

1. I don't want to go to the meeting. Besides, I'm _____ tired _____ go.
   - (A) too...to
   - (B) so...that
   - (C) such...that
   - (D) so...as to

2. The news that he wins the lottery is _____ good _____ be true.
   - (A) so...to
   - (B) so...that
   - (C) too...that
   - (D) too...to

解答： 　1. A　　2. D

翻譯練習題

1. 這電腦太重了，這小女孩抬不動。
2. 我媽媽擔心太多了，無法享受人生。

解答：

1. The computer is too heavy for the little girl to raise.
2. My mother worries too much to enjoy life.

關鍵句型 5：until的用法

【重點一】事 (肯定句) + **until** + N/句　　直到 …為止

例 Please wait until my husband comes home.
請等到我先生回家。
→[暗示我先生回家後就不用再等了。]

例 Mark was working for the hospital until 2009, when he got a job in America.
馬克為這家醫院一直工作到 2009 年，接着他在美國找到了一份工作。
→〔暗示在美國找到工作後就離開這家醫院了。〕

【重點二】事 (否定句) + until + N/句　直到…才

例 I didn't sleep until 11:30 p.m. the day before yesterday.
前天我到十一半點才睡覺.

例 According to my experience, don't jump to conclusions until you know everything.
根據我的經驗，直到你知道一切之前，別輕易下結論。

【提醒】 till = until　直到…為止

例 The stranger waited in front of my house till the policemen came.
那個陌生人在我家前面一直等到警察來。

例 The executive didn't leave the office till 10:00 p.m.
主管直到晚上十點才離開辦公室。

文法練習題

1. The police won't allow me to go away
   _____ I have told them what actually
   happened.
   (A) since
   (B) then
   (C) after
   (D) until

2. Every night my son studied hard and did
   his homework _____ 11:00 p.m.
   (A) at
   (B) since
   (C) until
   (D) for

解答： 1. D 2. C

翻譯練習題

1. 昨晚音樂會一直到作曲家抵達才開始。
2. 他在台北找到工作前，一直在台中工作。

解答：

1. Last night, the concert didn't begin until
   the composer arrived.
2. He worked in Taichung until he found a
   job in Taipei.

關鍵句型 6：it is + adj...

【重點一】 it is + adj... + to V

★ it is + adj (形容人的特質) + of 人 + to V

→adj (形容人的特質) = good/nice/kind/wise /foolish/bad/wrong/careful/polite

★ it is + adj (不可修飾個性) + for 動作者 + to V

→adj (不可修飾個性) = necessary/important/impossible

例 It's very kind of you to teach me English.
你真好，教我英文。

例 It is impossible for me to go on a date with him.
我不可能跟他約會。

【重點二】it + is + adj + that句
→[此句型的的 it = that 句,「it」為虛主詞,「that 句」為真主詞。]

it	be	good/nice	+ that 句	某事是好的
		possible/impossible		某事是可能的/不可能的
		surprising		某事是令人驚訝的
		amazing		某事是令人驚奇的
		wonderful		某事是令人驚嘆的、奇妙的
		apparent		某事是明顯的
		likely		某事是可能的
		lucky		某事是幸運的
		sad		某事是令人難過的
		certain		某事是確定的
		unbelievable		某事是難以置信的
		ridiculous		某事是荒謬的、可笑的
		understandable		某事是可以理解的

例 It's possible that she will not join in the activity.
她有可能不參加活動。

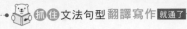

例 It is not surprising that you often talk much in a meeting.
你常常在會議上說太多，這不足為奇。

例 It was amazing that the little boy was able to play the guitar so well.
那小男孩那麼會彈吉他，真是令人驚奇。

例 It was apparent that he was not suitable for this job.
他顯然不適合這份工作。

例 It is likely that Vincent will be in Paris this winter.
今年冬天文生可能會在巴黎。

例 It is lucky that he was able to drive us home.
他能開車載我們回家，真幸運。

例 It's sad that you can't go with us.
你不能和我們一起去，真令人難過。

例 It is certain that he told a lie to us.
他對我們撒了謊，這是確定的。

【重點三】it + is + adj + that + S + (should) + V

→表示「主詞應該做些什麼事，但事實上卻還沒做」。

it	is	necessary	that + S + (should) + V	某事是必需的
		important		某事是重要的
		essential		某事是必要的
		imperative		某事是緊急的、極重要的
		vital		某事是極其重要的
		advisable		某事是明智的、可取的
		desirable		某事是值得做的、很可取

例 It is advisable that she (should) see a doctor.
她還是去看醫生比較好。

例 It is important that you (should) take exercise every day.
你應該要每天運動，這是很重要的。

例 It is necessary that you (should) speak English well in a foreign company.
在一家外商公司工作，你應該要很會說英文，這是必需的。

例 The child broke our window. It is essential that he (should) apologize to us.
這個小孩打破了我們的窗戶。他有必要跟我們道歉。

關鍵句型 7：人 + be + adj...

【重點一】人 + be + adj + that句

		convinced		某人深信某事
人	be	certain/sure	that 句	某人確定某事
		afraid		某人擔心某事
		confident		某人對某事有信心
		happy/glad		某人對某事感到開心、高興
		unhappy/sad		某人對某事感到不開心、難過
		lucky		某人在某事上是幸運的

例 I am convinced that he will tell the truth.
我確信他會説實話。

例 I am certain that she came here yesterday.
我確定她昨天有來這裡。

例 She was afraid that her husband might lose his job.
她擔心她先生會丟掉工作。

例 I'm confident that this film will be better than the previous one.
我有信心這部電影會比上一部更精彩。

例 I'm so happy that my boyfriend found a job at last.
我很高興我男友終於找到工作了。

例 She's sad that she broke up with her boyfriend last week.
上星期她跟男友分手了，她很難過。

例 He's lucky that he didn't miss the train.
他很幸運搭上火車。

【重點二】人 + is + adj + to V

人	be	likely	to V	某人可能…
		lucky		某人…是幸運的
		certain/sure		某人對某事感到確定
		happy/glad		某人對某事感到開心、高興
		unhappy/sad		某人對某事感到不開心、難過
		surprised/amazed/astonished		某人對某事物感到吃驚
		frustrated		某人對某事物感到沮喪

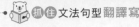

例 He is likely to enter an ideal university this autumn.
今年秋天他可能進入理想的大學就讀。

例 Mark was lucky enough to be selected for the volleyball team.
馬克真幸運,能被選入排球隊。

例 If I walk too fast, I am sure to fall.
如果我走太快,一定會跌倒。

例 She is happy to accept my invitation.
她很高興接受我的邀請。

例 I am sad to see them fight all day.
看到他們終日爭吵,我心裡很難過。

例 I was astonished to learn that he had failed in examination.
當我得知他考試不及格,我感到很吃驚。

例 I am frustrated to live in a country where people have no civil liberty.
生活在一個沒有公民自由的國家,我感到很沮喪。

【重點三】人 + is + adj + 介片

		convinced	of + N/V-ing	某人深信某事物
人	is	certain/ sure	of + N/V-ing about + N/ V-ing	某人對某事物感到確定、有把握
		afraid	of + N/V-ing	某人對某事物擔心
		confident	of + N/V-ing	某人對某事物有信心
		happy	about + N/V-ing with + N/V-ing	某人對某事物感到放心 某人對某事物感到滿意
		glad	about + N/V-ing of + N/V-ing	某人對某事物感到高興 某人對某事物感激
		unhappy/ sad	about + N/V-ing with + N/V-ing	某人對某事物感到不滿 某人對某事物感到不滿意
		surprised/ amazed/ astonished	at + N/V-ing	某人對某事物感到吃驚
		frustrated	with/at + N/V-ing	某人對某事物感到沮喪

例 The judge is convinced of her innocence.
法官非常相信她是無辜的。

例 You need to be sure of your abilities before making any decisions.
你在做出任何決定之前必須對自己的能力很有把握才行。

例 Are you quite sure about seeing the thief in the office last night? 你有很確定昨晚在辦公室看到小偷嗎？

例 I didn't tell my parents the truth because I was afraid of upsetting them.
我沒有告訴父母實話，因為我怕會讓他們不安。

例 My student Tom studies hard every day. He is confident of passing the examination.
我的學生湯姆每天用功讀書。他有信心通過考試。

例 Her parents are not happy about her living alone in Taipei.
她的父母對於她在台北一個人住很不放心。

例 Is my boss happy with my report?
老闆對我的報告感到滿意嗎？

例 Deep down my teacher felt glad about my performance.
對於我的表現我的老師發自內心地感到高興。

例 I like Jazz music a lot. I'll be glad of the new CD.
我很喜歡爵士樂。我會非常感謝這張新的CD。

例 The singer was unhappy about the press reports of the concert.
那位歌手對有關演唱會的新聞報導感到不滿。

例 If you're unhappy with your results, you can join in the speech contest next year.
你如果對成績不滿意，你可以明年再來參加演講比賽。

例 We were surprised at the old building's original condition.
我們驚訝地發現這棟舊公寓依然完好如初。

文法練習題

1. He fools around all day. _____ is not surprising that he can't find a job.
   (A) So
   (B) It
   (C) Which
   (D) That

2. I am surprised _____ learn that he lent so much money from you.
   (A) in
   (B) to
   (C) it
   (D) that

3. It is foolish _____ you to be addicted to wine.
   - (A) in
   - (B) to
   - (C) of
   - (D) for

4. He needs to be sure _____ her revolution before teaching her this difficult skill.
   - (A) in
   - (B) to
   - (C) of
   - (D) for

5. He often lies to us. I am afraid _____ he just didn't tell you the truth.
   - (A) in
   - (B) to
   - (C) of
   - (D) that

6. The doctor says it is necessary that my husband _____ an operation at once.
   - (A) has
   - (B) have
   - (C) had
   - (D) having

解答：1. B 2. B 3. C 4. C 5. D 6. B

翻譯練習題

1. 要鼓勵年輕的學生，有時候買一些小禮物給他們是需要的。
2. 你在教室裡抽菸是不好的。
3. 王老師對於我的期中考成績感到不滿。
4. 她今天下午可能會跟你去看電影。
5. 我有信心她會接受我的邀請。
6. 你應該去熟悉你的學習環境，這對你很有益處。

　　【用 It is desirable that...】

解答：

1. To encourage young students, it is sometimes necessary that you buy some little gifts for them.
2. It's bad of you to smoke in the classroom.
3. Mr. Wang was not happy about the score of my mid-term exam.
4. She is likely to go to the movies with you this afternoon.
   = It is likely that she will go to the movies with you this afternoon.
5. I am confident of her accepting my invitation.
   = I am confident that she will accept my invitation.
6. It is desirable that you (should) have some familiarity with your learning environment. It's good for you.

關鍵句型 8：it is + known/believed/said/reported/ found

★ it is + known/believed/said/reported/found
+ that 句
= S (非it) + is + known/believed/said/reported/
found + to V
據聞/據信/據說/據報導/據發現…

【注意】如動作有先後之別，要用 **to have pp**

例 It is said that Columbus discovered the America.

= Columbus is said <u>to have discovered</u> America.
據說哥倫布發現了美洲。

例 It is said that the superstar from Hong Kong is the first one to use the room.

= The superstar from Hong Kong is said to be the first one to use the room.
據說來自香港的巨星是第一位使用這個房間的人。

例 It is believed that this child has magic power to communicate with ghosts.

= The child is believed to have magic power to communicate with ghosts.
據信這小孩具有神奇的能力能和鬼魂溝通。

文法練習題

1. You'd better bring an umbrella with you.
   It is reported ____ it might rain this evening.
   - (A) that
   - (B) to
   - (C) of
   - (D) which

2. Hsimending (西門町) is believed ____ a popular place for teens in Taipei.
   - (A) that is
   - (B) to have
   - (C) to be
   - (D) being

解答：　**1. A**　　**2. C**

翻譯練習題

1. 據說他晚上比白天有活力。
2. 據聞，這間博物館以古畫聞名。

解答：

1. It is said that he has more energy in the night than in the day.
   = He is said to have more energy in the night than in the day.
2. It is said that the museum is famous for old paintings.

= The museum is said to be famous for old paintings.

關鍵句型 9：one, the other, another, some, others, the others

【重點一】

★ one...the other (只有兩者)

★ one...another (不只兩者)

★ one...another....the other (有三者)
　→三者以上 one...another...another...
　　another...最後一個才是 the other

例 One of my parents is a guitarist, and the other is a singer.
我的雙親中一位是吉他手，另一位是歌手。

例 The audience in the concert hall left one after another.
音樂廳裡的觀眾一個接著一個離開了。

例 I saw three boxes on the desk. One is large, another is medium, and the other is small.
我在桌上看到三個盒子。一個是大的，一個是中的，一個是小的。

例 I have 5 pens. One is red, another is black, another is yellow, another is green, and the other is blue.
我有五支筆。一支是紅色的，一支是黑色

的，一支是黃色的，一支是綠色的，最後一支是藍色的。

【重點二】from one + 單數名詞 + to another
[= from + N + to + N]
從…到…

例 Birth rates vary from one country to another.
= Birth rates vary from country to country.
出生率因國而異。

【重點三】某一全體中的「一些」

★ one..., another..., another..., and the others
(the others 表有範圍限制的最後幾個)

★ some..., others..., others..., and the others
(the others 表有範圍限制的最後一些、剩餘的全部)

★ some...others (some)...others (some)...and still others...

（一些…，一些…，一些…，還有一些…）

（用於數個部分之情境，沒數完全體）

例 I have 8 pens. One is red, another is black, and the others are blue.
我有八支筆。一支是紅色的，一支是黑色的，其他六支是藍色的。

例 <u>Some</u> products make our lives convenient, while <u>others</u> make our lives more dangerous.

有些產品讓我們的生活便利,而有些則使我們的生活更危險。

例 When I stepped into the classroom, <u>some</u> students were studying, <u>others</u> were listening to music, <u>and the others</u> were chatting.

當我踏進教室時,有些學生在讀書,有些則在聽音樂,剩下的其他學生在聊天。

例 At the beach, <u>some</u> are sunbathing, <u>others</u> (=some) are swimming, <u>others</u> (=some) are playing the guitar, <u>and still others</u> are playing volleyball.

沙灘上有些人在做日光浴,有些人在游泳,有些人在彈吉他,還有些人在打排球。

文法練習題

1. In this fancy restaurant, you can watch a guitarist pass _____ singing sentimental love songs.

   (A) from one to another table

   (B) from one table to another

   (C) from table to another

   (D) from one to table

2. To relax, some people like to exercise, while ＿＿ prefer to sleep.
   (A) others
   (B) the other
   (C) another
   (D) the others

3. There are many animals in the zoo, including elephants, giraffes, zebras, monkeys, snakes and bears. Some were tame, ＿＿ were ferocious, and still others were indifferent.
   (A) other
   (B) others
   (C) the others
   (D) another

解答： 1. B   2. A   3. B

翻譯練習題

1. 莎莉的朋友中有些去玩球，其餘的朋友則在沙灘上做日光浴。
2. 我看見六件毛衣。兩件紅，四件紫。
   【請練習用 the others 來替換】
3. 教室裡有些學生在閱讀，有些則在睡覺，還有些在聊天。

解答：

1. Some of Sally's friends played balls, and the others sunbathed on the beach.

2. I saw six sweaters. Two are red, and four are purple.

   (= I saw six sweaters. Two are red, and the others are purple. = I saw six sweaters. Two of the sweaters are red and the others are purple. = I saw six sweaters. Two of them are red and the others are purple.)

3. In the classroom some students are reading, others are sleeping, and still others are chatting.

關鍵句型 10：代替名詞

【重點一】特定與不特定

one	代替不特定的單數名詞
ones	代替不特定的複數名詞
it	代替特定的單數名詞
them	代替特定的複數名詞

★the one／the ones + adj子句／介片

例 Do you have a dictionary? I need to borrow one.

你有字典嗎？我需要借一本。

→one 代替 a dictionary，沒有特定要哪一本字典，只要可以借到一本就好。

例 Give me pens. I want blue <u>ones</u>.
給我筆。我要藍色的。

　→ones 代替 pens，沒有特定要哪幾隻藍
　　色的筆，只要藍色的即可。

例 A: Do you want to buy this book?
　B: Yes, I want to buy <u>it</u>.
　A：你要買這本書嗎？
　B：是的，我要買下。

　→it 代替 this book，就是這本，而不是其
　　他本。

例 She can't find her books. She forgets where
　she put <u>them</u>.
　她找不到她的書。她忘了放在哪裡了。

　→them 代替 her books，就是她的書，而
　　不是其他的書。

例 This book is heavier than <u>the one</u> which
　you hold in your hand.
　這本書比你手裡拿著的那一本還要重。

例 The hardest goodbyes are <u>the ones</u> that you
　don't get
　ready to say.
　最難的道別是那些你還沒有準備好要說
　的。

【重點二】表「全無」時

兩者用 **neither**	+ 單數動詞
三者以上用 **none**	

★在日常英語口語中，當 **none of** 後面跟複數名詞時，動詞常用複數形式：**None of us like to read this book.**
我們沒有人喜歡讀這本書。

例 Neither of my children has visited the park yet.
我的兩個小孩都還沒參觀過這個公園。

例 None of the machines is in operation yet.
還沒有一個機器在運作。

【重點三】不定代名詞

someone/somebody something	某人 某事	
everyone/everybody everything	每個人 每件事， 一切事物	+形容詞 【後位修飾】
anyone/anybody anything	任何人 任何事	
no one/nobody nothing	沒有人 無事、無物	

例 I feel nervous. Could you tell me something interesting?

我感到緊張。可以告訴我一些有趣的事情嗎？

例 I am fond of eating <u>anything delicious</u>.
我喜歡吃任何美味的東西。

例 Is there <u>anything else</u> we need to discuss tonight?
今晚還有我們需要討論的事情嗎？

【重點四】前者……後者……

the former/the latter	可表單複數	可指人或事物
the one/the other	只表單數	可指人或事物
that/this	只表單數	不能指人
those/these	只表複數	不能指人

例 Students may be divided into two different kinds, namely, the idlers and the bookworms. <u>The former</u> don't like to study. <u>The latter</u> are seldom absent.
學生也許可分為兩類，就是懶蟲和書蟲。前者不愛唸書。後者很少缺課。

例 I have two cars: a white one and a black one; <u>the one</u> is more expensive than <u>the other</u>.
我有兩輛車子：一輛白色、一輛黑色；白色的比黑色的要來得貴。

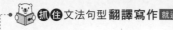

例 Health is more important than wealth; that (= the former) is the basis of this (= the latter).

健康比財富重要,前者是後者的基礎。

例 I like dogs better than cats; those (= the former) are more loyal than these (= the latter).

我較喜歡狗而較不喜歡貓;前者比後者更忠心。

文法練習題

1. Miss Ho gave me a black pen yesterday, and today she gave me a red _____.
   - (A) one
   - (B) ones
   - (C) it
   - (D) them

2. She doesn't realize that she means more to me than _____.
   - (A) else anything
   - (B) anything else
   - (C) nothing
   - (D) neither

3. Neither of his two daughters _____ married yet.
   - (A) get
   - (B) are

(C) have got

(D) has got

解答： 1. A　2. B　3. D

翻譯練習題

1. 她的三個兒子都還沒有從大學畢業。
2. 她沒有新的裙子，她只有舊的。
3. 工作與玩樂對我來說都是必需的。前者會給我精力，後者會給我休息。(用 the former...the latter...)

解答：

1. None of her three sons has graduated from university yet.
2. She has no new skirts. She has only old ones.
3. Work and play are both necessary to me. The former gives me energy, and the latter gives me rest.

關鍵句型 11：代替整句

★ it/that/this 可以代替前面提過的一件事

例 I did not trust him. This made him very angry.

我不信任他。這使他非常生氣。

→本例句中 this 代替前面的「I did not trust him.」

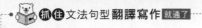

例 He is selfish. <u>That</u> is why his co-workers don't like him.

他很自私。那就是他的同事不喜歡他的原因。

→本例句中 that 代替前面的「He is selfish.」

例 She will not join our guitar club. <u>It</u> makes us disappointed.

她不會加入我們的吉他社。這讓我們很失望。

→本例句中 it 代替前面的「She will not join our guitar club.」

【注意】準關係代名詞也可以代替整句

★句, which/as + 不完整句.

= As + 不完整句, 句.

例 Miss Ho takes care of her students, <u>which</u> is her daily responsibility.

= Miss Ho takes care of her students, <u>as</u> is her daily responsibility.

= <u>As</u> is Miss Ho's daily responsibility, she takes care of her students.

何老師照顧她的學生,這是她每日的責任。

→which/as 代替的是這個句子:「Miss Ho takes care of her students.」

文法練習題

1. The president will attend the meeting tomorrow. _____makes everybody nervous.
   - (A) Which
   - (B) What
   - (C) It
   - (D) They

2. Mark has always got good grades on math examinations, _____ has made him the envy of his classmates.
   - (A) which
   - (B) what
   - (C) it
   - (D) that

解答： 1. C   2. A

翻譯練習題

1. 在安靜的環境中睡覺會幫助你放鬆。
2. 我沒有聽從父親的忠告，讓他非常生氣。

解答：

1. Sleep in a guiet environment, which will help you to relax.
2. I did not follow/take my father's advice. This/That/It made him very angry.

關鍵句型 12：as far as + S + V　就某人所、而…

★As far as + 句, 句.

= 句, as far as + 句.

as far as + 句	中文意思
as far as one knows as far as one is aware	就某人所知
as far as one can recall	就某人所能回憶
as far as one can go	就某人所能及
as far as one can see as far as the eye can see	就某人所見 放眼所見
as far as one is concerned	就某人而言
as far as it is possible	盡可能地

例 As far as I know, she is a very responsible teacher.

就我所知，她是一個非常盡責的老師。

例 As far as we're concerned, it is important to finish the project before the deadline.

就我們而言，期限之前完成這件企劃是重要的。

例 The problem lies in his laziness, as far as I can see.
在我看來，問題出在他的懶惰。

文法練習題

1. The doctor promised me to save the little girl _____ it is possible.
   - (A) as far as
   - (B) even though
   - (C) so that
   - (D) however

2. This novel is not bad as far as the plot _____, but it lacks content.
   - (A) can see
   - (B) is possible
   - (C) concerning
   - (D) is concerned

解答：　**1. A**　　**2. D**

翻譯練習題

1. 就我而言，他說的話很重要。
2. 放眼望去，平原上盡是各式各樣的動物。

解答：

1. As far as I am concerned, what he says/ said is important.

2. There are a variety of animals on the plain as far as the eye can see.

關鍵句型 13：as + adj/adv + as

【重點一】as + adj/adv + as
　　　　　像…一樣的…

例 The painting is as beautiful as a star-filled sky.
這幅畫有如滿天星空般的美麗。

例 My grandfather can't walk as fast as he used to.
我的祖父走路不像以前那樣快。

【重點二】as + adj/adv + as S can
　　　　　= as + adj/adv + as possible
　　　　　盡可能地…

例 She wants to become a dancer and is training herself as hard as she can.
她要做舞者，正下苦功盡力自我訓練。

例 As a scholar, he must try to acquire as much knowledge as possible.
身為一名學者，他必須盡可能地獲得大量的知識。

文法練習題

1. Don't be late. Come as soon _____ you can.
   - (A) as
   - (B) that
   - (C) the same
   - (D) if

2. She wishes she were _____ the superstar.
   - (A) much beautiful than
   - (B) more beautiful as
   - (C) as beautiful as
   - (D) as beautifully as

解答：　　1. A　　2. C

翻譯練習題

1. 王老師要求我儘快跟我父母聯繫。
2. 我母親跟蜜蜂一樣忙碌，因為她每天都有很多事要做。

解答：

1. Mr. Wang asked me to get in touch with my parents as soon as possible.
   (= Mr. Wang asked me to get in touch with my parents as soon as I can.)

2. My mother is as busy as a bee because she has a lot of things to do every day.

關鍵句型 14：現在分詞和過去分詞當形容詞用

★現在分詞和過去分詞當形容詞用，可分兩種：

1. 一般動詞而來：V-ing (主動)／pp (被動)
2. 情緒動詞而來：
   V-ing (令別人感到…的)／pp (自己感到…的)

【重點一】「一般動詞」而來的現在分詞和過去分詞當形容詞用

1. 現在分詞 (V-ing) + 名詞 【現在分詞 (V-ing) 表主動】
2. 過去分詞 (pp) + 名詞 【過去分詞 (pp) 表被動】

例 The barking dog is fierce. 那隻吠叫的狗很兇猛。

　→【barking 為動詞 bark 的現在分詞，當形容詞用，修飾 dog】

例 The broken vase is expensive. 這破損的花瓶很貴。

　→【broken 為動詞 break 的過去分詞，當形容詞用，修飾 vase】

【重點二】「情緒動詞」而來的現在分詞和過去
分詞當形容詞用

1. 常見的情緒動詞如下表：

情緒動詞 (原形)	現在分詞 (V-ing)	過去分詞 (pp)
surprise (驚訝)	surprising	surprised
confuse (困惑)	confusing	confused
excite (興奮)	exciting	excited
bore (無聊)	boring	bored
interest (興趣)	interesting	interested
scare (驚嚇、恐懼)	scaring	scared
terrify (害怕、驚恐)	terrifying	terrified

2. 「情緒動詞」的現在分詞 (V-ing) 修飾
「事物」，意思為「令人感到…」。
「情緒動詞」的過去分詞 (pp) 修飾
「人」，意思為「感到…」。

例 This is an interesting book.
這是一本有趣的書。

→【interesting 為情緒動詞 interest 的現在
分詞，當形容詞用，修飾 book，意思
是「令人感到有趣的」】

例 I am interested in Japanese.
我對日文感興趣。

→【interested 為情緒動詞 interest 的過去
分詞，當形容詞用，修飾 I (我)，意思
是「感到興趣的」】

文法練習題

1. My son was bitten by our neighbor's dog
   when he was very young and he was
   very _____ of dogs from then on.
   (A) scare
   (B) scared
   (C) scary
   (D) scaring

2. This delicate cup had been kept in the
   cupboard so that it wouldn't get _____.
   (A) break
   (B) broke
   (C) broken
   (D) breaking

解答：　**1. B**　　**2. C**

翻譯練習題

1. 約翰悄悄地走進房間，親了他睡覺中的
   太太。
2. 那些說明模糊不清，我不知道如何安裝
   這個軟體。

解答：

1. John crept into the room and kissed his sleeping wife.
2. The instructions were so confusing that I didn't know

   how to install this software.

關鍵句型 15：複合形容詞

複合形容詞	組成解說	例子	中文意思
adj-感官動詞ing	常見的感官動詞為：look/ taste/ smell/ hear	a good-looking star good-tasting tea	一個好看的明星 好喝的茶
N-Ving	N 為 Ving 的受詞	many award-winning stories a breath-taking painting English-speaking countries a heart-breaking accident	許多得獎的故事 令人讚嘆的畫 說英文的國家 令人心碎的意外
N-pp	被修飾的 N 為 pp 的受詞	hand-made cookies a hand-written letter semi-fermented tea leaves	手工製的餅乾 一封手寫的信 半發酵的茶葉

adv-pp	被修飾N 為pp 的受詞	a well-behaved teacher a newly-built building a beautifully-dressed singer a much-praised performance now-unwanted coins	一位行為端正的 老師 一棟新蓋的建築 物 一個打扮漂亮的 歌手 一個備受讚揚的 表演 現在不要的 硬幣
adj-pp	被修飾 的N完成 了動作 或被完 成了	the new-fallen leaves the beautiful-painted rock	剛落下的葉子 美麗繪圖的 岩石
adj- Ned	N為被修 飾N的一 部分	my red-haired grandmother a blue-colored car	我的紅髮 祖母 一台藍色的 車子
數字- 單位		a 400-meter race a two-day trip	四百公尺賽跑 兩天的旅行

例 This novel is about a heart-breaking love triangle.

這本小說是關於一段令人心碎的三角戀愛。

例 As we waited, a well-mannered waiter came and asked us what we would like to order.

當我們在等待的時候，一個有禮貌的服務生過來問我們要點什麼。

例 The popular star entered a <u>red-colored</u> car and left the spot.
那個受歡迎的明星進入一台紅色的車子，然後離開現場。

例 The athlete won the 100-meter race with a time of 11.30 seconds.
那個運動員以十一秒半的成績贏得了一百公尺賽跑。

文法練習題

1. There are a wide variety of ingredients available to make _____ soaps.
   - (A) making-hand
   - (B) hand-make
   - (C) hand-making
   - (D) hand-made

2. This company lets you buy a _____ home with a deposit of only 5% of the purchase price.
   - (A) new-build
   - (B) new-building
   - (C) newly-built
   - (D) newly-building

解答： **1. D**　　**2. C**

翻譯練習題

1. 我們正計劃開車到宜蘭玩兩天。
2. 破紀錄的熱流上周引發了森林火災。

解答：

1. We are planning a two-day trip to Ilan by car.
2. A record-breaking heat wave sparked forest fires last week.

關鍵句型 16：the + adj

★the + adj

→表某一群體 (= adj + people)

	形容詞	同義片語	中文意思
the	**blind**	= blind people	盲者
	crippled	= crippled people	殘障者
	disabled	= disabled people	殘疾者
	elderly	= elderly people	老者
	lonely	= lonely people	孤者
	poor	= poor people	貧窮者
	rich	= rich people	富有者
	sick	= sick people	病者

例 He is a kind man. He is gentle to the elderly, he cares for the sick, and he shows respect for the poor.

他是一個善良的人。他以慈愛對待老者，

關心病人，也尊重貧窮者。

文法練習題

1. He received an honor for his devotion to
   helping ＿＿＿ through education.
   (A) poor
   (B) poor man
   (C) the poor
   (D) poverty

2. The museum has good access for ＿＿＿.
   (A) disable
   (B) disabled
   (C) the disabled
   (D) unable person

解答：　　1. C　　2. C

翻譯練習題

1. 在台灣老年照護有區域性的差異嗎？
2. 這個學生因為發明了一個幫助盲人的設
   備而得到了國家志工獎。

解答：

1. Do regional differences exist with respect to the care for the elderly in Taiwan?

2. The student won a national volunteer award for creating a device to help the blind.

關鍵句型 17：go + adj

★**go + adj** (通常是意思上「比較負面的」形容詞)

→表示「變成…狀態」

	負面形容詞	中文意思
go	**astray**	入歧途、迷失
	bankrupt	破產
	crazy	發瘋
	rotten	腐敗
	sour	變酸、壞掉
	wrong	不對勁、有問題

例 Students who fail in their academic studies may easily go astray.
學業失敗的學生也許容易誤入歧途。

例 Some of the apples went completely rotten.
有些蘋果完全腐爛了。

例 He went bankrupt several times before he built this company.

在建立這家公司之前他破產了好幾次。

文法練習題

1. Don't use cream that has gone _____ in cooking.
   - (A) spoil
   - (B) decay
   - (C) rot
   - (D) sour

2. When everything seems to be _____, she still feels
   confident of herself.
   - (A) gone wrong
   - (B) go wrongly
   - (C) going wrong
   - (D) going wrongly

解答： **1. D** **2. C**

翻譯練習題

1. 我很難過聽到他的生意失敗了，也破產了。

2. 我覺得我無法及時完成這個企劃。我快要發瘋了。

解答：

1. I am sorry to hear that his business failed and he went bankrupt.

2. I think I can't finish the project in time. I am going crazy.

關鍵句型 18：形容詞比較級／副詞比較級的加強

★far/much/still/even/a lot/a great deal

+ adj比較級／adv比較級

→形容詞比較級／副詞比較級的加強
【…多了】

例 He is <u>much</u> more independent than his younger sister.

他比他妹妹獨立多了

例 Telling the truth is <u>a lot</u> better than making excuses.

說實話比找藉口好太多了。

例 You'll get to my office <u>far</u> more quickly by MRT.

你坐捷運到我辦公室就快多了。

文法練習題

1. It's hot today. Will it be _____ tomorrow?

(A) the same hot

(B) as hotter

(C) more hotter
(D) still hotter

2. The first question is very difficult, yet the second one is _____ easier.

(A) much

(B) many

(C) more

(D) most

解答：**1. D　2. A**

翻譯練習題

1. 比股票市場還要危險得多的是你的貪婪。
2. 住在合理距離的農夫可以更加即時地將他們的蔬菜水果送到市場。

解答：

1. What's even more dangerous than the stock market is your greediness.

2. The farmers who live within a reasonable distance can send their vegetables and fruits to markets far more promptly.

關鍵句型 19：動作當主詞，要改為不定詞或動名詞

★動作當主詞，要改為不定詞（to + V）或動名詞
（V-ing），一般而言，不定詞表「未來或目的」，動名詞表「經驗」。

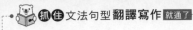

★不論是不定詞（to + V）或動名詞（V-ing）
　當主詞，要視為一件事情，後面要用「單數
　動詞」。

★不定詞（to + V）當主詞時，也可放在句
　尾，前面用虛主詞「it」代替。

例 Playing the piano has become her hobby.
　彈鋼琴已經變成她的嗜好。

例 To find a good job is my next goal.
　= It is my next goal to find a good job.
　找份好工作是我下一個目標。

文法練習題

1. _____ is quite useful for me to contact
　with my
　customers who live far away.
　(A) Use e-mails
　(B) Using e-mails
　(C) It uses e-mails
　(D) By using e-mails

2. Is it possible for you _____ some of
　your pocket money aside for movie-
　going?
　(A) set
　(B) sets
　(C) to set
　(D) setting

解答：1. B　　2. C

翻譯練習題

1. 請朋友吃飯卻沒錢付帳是件尷尬的事情。
2. 收集郵票在我家是最受歡迎的嗜好。

解答：

1. It is embarrassing to treat your friend to a meal without the money to pay for it.
2. Stamp collecting is the most popular hobby in my family.

關鍵句型 20：不定詞或動名詞作「受詞」

【重點一】不定詞作「受詞」，常放在句尾，前面用虛受詞「it」代替

	believe			
	think			
	regard			
主詞	consider	it	adj／N	to V
	find			
	make			
	take			

例 I think it easy to fix this bicycle.
　我覺得修理這台腳踏車很容易。

例 This digital camera makes it fun to visually explore the room.
這台數位相機讓視覺地探索這個房間成為樂趣。

例 In most cases, students regard it a burden to organize ideas in given structures and formats.
大多數情況下，學生認為用既定的結構跟格式來組織想法是一種負擔。

例 I believe it dangerous to leave your engine running during refueling.
我相信加油時沒關掉引擎是危險的。

【重點二】動名詞作「受詞」，放在「及物動詞」及「介係詞」後面

主詞	Vt	V-ing
	Vi + 介係詞	V-ing

例 After he admitted stealing the money, he was punished.
在他承認偷錢後，他受到了處罰。

例 He will insist on brushing his teeth just when I want to have a bath.
正當我要洗澡的時候，他偏要去刷牙。

文法練習題

1. I don't think it's necessary _____ a person by his past.
   - (A) judge
   - (B) judging
   - (C) to judge
   - (D) that judges

2. I find _____ interesting to see how designers develop their concepts.
   - (A) it
   - (B) that
   - (C) which
   - (D) what

解答：　**1. C**　**2. A**

翻譯練習題

1. 承蒙邀請赴宴她深感榮幸。
2. 交戰雙方仍未順利達成協議。

解答：

1. She considers it a great honor to be invited to the banquet.
2. The warring parties have not yet succeeded in reaching an agreement.

四、認識特殊句型的使用

關鍵句型 1：名詞片語

★ 名詞片語

→[功能：當 S 或 O]

where/when/how/why/whether + to V [不缺O]

what/who(m)/which + to V [缺O]

例 Hi, Miss Lin! Can you tell me <u>when to leave for Paris</u>?

嗨，林小姐！可以告訴我何時要前往巴黎嗎？

例 She was upset over her illness. She asked me <u>whom to talk to about it.</u>

她為她的病而憂心忡忡。她問我要跟誰講。

文法練習題

1. The little boy is lost; he doesn't know _____.

(A) where does he go

(B) where he goes

(C) where to go

(D) where should he go

2. I was so nervous that I did not know
_____ to do.
   (A) where
   (B) when
   (C) how
   (D) what

解答：　　1. C　　2. D

翻譯練習題

1. 你必須馬上決定參不參加這個聚會。
2. 有些學生不曉得如何使用字典。

解答：

1. You have to decide whether or not to go to
   the party at once.
2. Some students do not know how to use
   a dictionary.

關鍵句型 2：名詞子句化簡為名詞片語

★如果主要句中的S，等於名詞子句中的S，
　名詞子句可化簡為名詞片語：

1. 去掉名詞子句的S
2. 去掉助動詞
3. 動詞改為不定詞(to + V)

例 We should find out what we should do to
　 help stray dogs.

= We should find out what to do to help stray
　 dogs.

我們應該設法幫助流浪狗。

→[第一步,去掉 we。第二步,去掉 should。第三步,do 改為 to do。]

例 Have you decided <u>whether you should buy the house yet</u>?

= Have you decided <u>whether to buy the house yet</u>?

你決定好要買這間房子了嗎?

→[第一步,去掉you。第二步,去掉 should。第三步,buy改為to buy。]

文法練習題

1. The interviewer asked the female interviewee _____ he should hire her.

   (A) what

   (B) who

   (C) why

   (D) that

2. As you proceed along life's journey, you must learn

   when and how _____ cast off your shortcomings.

   (A) to

   (B) should

   (C) it

   (D) that

解答： **1. C**　　**2. A**

翻譯練習題

1. 我媽媽知道明天放學後她該何時來接我。
   【用名詞子句及名詞片語，兩種答案】
2. 要買哪一本書才好，我需要一些指點。
   【用名詞子句及名詞片語，兩種答案】

解答：

1. My mother knows when she should pick
   me up after school tomorrow.

   = My mother knows when to pick me up
   after school tomorrow.

2. I need some advice on which book I
   should buy.

   = I need some advice on which book to buy.

關鍵句型 3：分詞構句

★兩句在一起，沒有連接詞，可將其中一句改
為分詞構句。步驟如下：

1. 去同 S /不同則不去掉
2. 動詞改為現在分詞 (V-ing)
3. 如果此現在分詞是 being，則可省 (也可
   不省)
   →[不省的話強調「原因」]

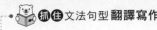

【提醒】以「後句」進行分詞構句，前後兩個動作有「同時進行」之意。

例 He lay on the bed. He listened to his favorite music.

→He lay on the bed <u>and</u> listened to his favorite music.

→He lay on the bed, <u>listening</u> to his favorite music.

[第一步去掉he, 第二步listened改成 listening]

他躺在床上聽最喜歡的音樂。

→[lay 和 listened 有同時進行之意]

【提醒】以「前句」進行分詞構句，前後兩個動作有「先後發生，或因果」之意。

例 The student finished the exam. Then he went home.

→<u>After</u> the student finished the exam, he went home.

→<u>Finishing</u> the exam, the student went home.

[第一步去掉the student, 第二步finished改成 finishing]

考完試後，那個學生就回家。

→[finished 和 went 有先後發生之意]

例 The weather was fine. We went mountain-climbing last Sunday.

→Because the weather was fine, we went mountain-climbing last Sunday.

→The weather being fine, we went mountain-climbing last Sunday.

[兩句主詞不同不能去掉S，直接跳到第二步「was 改成 being」，being 保留，強調及表示「原因」]

因為天氣很好，上週日我們去爬山。

→[以「前句」進行分詞構句，前後兩句為「因果」關係]

文法練習題

1. When she was a third grader, she was caught _____ in the test by using a calculator.
   (A) cheat
   (B) cheats
   (C) cheating
   (D) she cheated

2. _____ her letter, he wrote a note in reply, and put the note in an envelope.
   (A) Received
   (B) He received
   (C) Receiving
   (D) Being received

解答： **1. C**　　**2. C**

翻譯練習題

1. 在一個寒冷的冬日傍晚，那個老婦人站在門邊，在想念她的先生。【用分詞構句】

2. 因為活力充沛，崔西狗狗總是愛玩耍。【用分詞構句】

解答：

1. On a cold winter evening, the old lady stood by the door, missing her husband.

2. Being an energetic dog, Tracy is playful all the time.

關鍵句型 4：副詞子句簡化的分詞構句

副詞子句中的主詞如果和主要子句的主詞相同者，可以進行分詞構句的化簡，步驟如下：

1. 去同主詞 (副詞子句裡)

2. 動詞改為現在分詞 (V-ing)

3. 如果此現在分詞是 **being**，則可省。→[不省的話強調「原因」]

例 While we were crossing the street, we ran into Miss Ho.

= While crossing the street, we ran into Miss Ho.

當我們過街時，我們碰到了何老師。

→[1. 去同主詞 we。2. 動詞 were 改為現

在分詞 being。 3. being 省略。】

例 He will study hard <u>if he is encouraged</u> by his teachers.

= He will study hard <u>if encouraged</u> by his teachers.

他的老師鼓勵他的話,他會用功讀書的。

→[1. 去同主詞 he。2. 動詞 is 改為現在分詞 being。 3. being 省略。]

例 Please be polite <u>when you make</u> a request.

= Please be polite <u>when making</u> a request.

當你有所請求時,請有禮貌。

→[1. 去同主詞 you。2. 動詞 make 改為現在分詞 making。]

【提醒】如果是 **because** 副詞子句,化簡後連 **because** 都去掉。可保留 **being** 來強調「原因」。

例 <u>Because she was surprised</u> by what her boyfriend had said, she dropped the flowers in her hands.

= <u>(Being) surprised</u> by what her boyfriend had said, she dropped the flowers in her hands.

因為驚訝於她男友所說的話,她手上的花掉了下來。

→[1. 去同主詞 she。2. 動詞 was 改為現在分詞 being。 3. being 可省略,也可不省,不省的話強調「原因」。

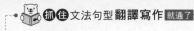

4. because 省略。]

文法練習題

1. After ____ with the school psychologist,
   Lisa felt more confident.
   (A) talked
   (B) talks
   (C) talking
   (D) she talks

2. ____ on a trip, she always has her camera
   ready.
   (A) In case of
   (B) While
   (C) As
   (D) During

解答： 1. C 2. B

翻譯練習題

1. 昨晚我奶奶在看電視時睡著了。【用
   While + V-ing...】
2. 因為不知道該說些什麼，肇事者保持沉
   默。
   【用副詞子句簡化的分詞構句】

解答:

1. While watching TV last night, my grand-mother fell asleep.
2. Not knowing what to say, the culprit remained silent.

關鍵句型 5:倒裝句

一般句子結構	相對應的倒裝句
S + Vi + 介片/adv	= 介片/adv + Vi + S (非代名詞).
S + be + 非名詞.	= 非名詞 + be + S (非代名詞).
句 + **only** + 介片/adv	= **Only** + 介片/adv + 倒裝句. [倒裝方法: **(1)** 助動詞 + S **(2)** be + S **(3)** do/does/did + S + 一般動詞]
否定句, **and** 否定句, **either.**	= 否定句, **and neither** + 肯定倒裝句. = 否定句, **nor** + 肯定倒裝句. [倒裝方法: **(1)** 助動詞 + S **(2)** be + S **(3)** do/does/did + S + 一般動詞]
肯定句, **and** 肯定句, **too.**	= 肯定句, **and so** + 肯定倒裝句. [倒裝方法: **(1)** 助動詞 + S **(2)** be + S **(3)** do/does/did + S + 一般動詞]

例 A student + sat (vi.) + in front of the table (介片).

= In front of the table sat a student.
一位學生坐在桌子前面。

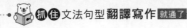

例 A small stream is in front of our house.
= In front of our house is a small stream.
我家門前有一條小溪。

例 She could talk to me only then (adv.那時).
= Only + then + could she talk to me.
她只有那時候才可以跟我說話。

例 The watchdog was able to scare the thief away only by barking.
= Only + by barking + was the watchdog able to scare the thief away.
只有藉由吠叫，那隻守衛犬才可以把小偷嚇跑。

例 He feels good only by making a lot of money.
= Only + by making a lot of money + does he feel good.
只有藉著賺很多錢，他才覺得滿意。

例 William has never been to London, and Jane has (助動詞) never been (pp) there, either.
=William has never been to London, and neither has Jane.
= William has never been to London, nor has Jane.
威廉沒有去過倫敦，珍也沒有。

例 Most people make New Year resolutions on New Year's Day, and we do, too.

= Most people make New Year resolutions on New Year's Day, and so do we.
大多數人都在新年立下新年決心，而我們也是。

【提醒】這邊的**do**為助動詞，代替動詞片語 **make New Year resolutions**。

文法練習題

1. Only by making changes will it _____ possible for our company to make profits.
   (A) but also
   (B) hence
   (C) then
   (D) be

2. We didn't want to make friends with them, _____ to talk to us.
   (A) and nor they want
   (B) nor it was possible
   (C) nor did they want
   (D) and either do they want

解答： **1. D**　　**2. C**

翻譯練習題

1. 綠意不長久,美麗的花也是。
   【用 nor...】
2. 他坐在一片漆黑中,那時他才意識到自己是多麼的寂寞。【用 only then...】

解答:

1. The green does not stay long, nor does the beautiful flower.
2. He sat in the dark; only then did he realize how lonely he was.

關鍵句型 6:強調句型

It	is/was	被強調的字 (N)	who(m) (前面的字是人) which (前面的字是物) that (前面的字,不論是人或物,都可以用)	餘句
		被強調的片語	that	
		被強調的副詞子句	that	

例 [原句] But here my manager's word counts.
但是在這裡我經理的話算數。

→[強調句] But here it's my manager's word which counts.

= But here it's my manager's word that counts.
但是在這裡是我經理的話才算數。

例 [原句] Her mother moved three times <u>for her children</u>.

她媽媽為了小孩搬家三次。

→[強調句] It was <u>for her children</u> <u>that</u> her mother moved three times.

她媽媽是為了小孩才搬家三次的。

例 [原句] <u>Before you got home</u>, a boy broke the window.

你回家之前，一個男孩打破了窗戶。

→[強調句] It was <u>before you got home</u> that a boy broke the window.

是在你回家之前，一個男孩打破了窗戶的。

文法練習題

1. In Western culture it is one's individuality _____ is emphasized.

(A) but

(B) then

(C) what

(D) that

2. _____ was after his wife left that he realized how important she meant to him.

(A) It

(B) When

(C) What

(D) Only

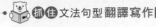

解答： 1. D 　　2. A

翻譯練習題

1. 這個戒指他是為了女友才買的。[用強調句型]
2. 萬事起頭難。[用強調句型]

解答：

1. It was for his girlfriend that he bought the ring.
2. It is the first step which/that is troublesome.

關鍵句型 7：不是A而是B

★ not A but B 　不是A而是B

→ AB 詞性、結構要相等

例 He is not + fat (adj) + but + thin (adj).
他不胖，而是瘦。

例 They left for Taipei + not + by train (介片) + but + by bus (介片).
他們不是搭火車去台北，而是搭客運。

例 It is + not + what you say (名詞子句) + but + what you do (名詞子句) + that counts.
重要的不是你說了什麼，而是你做了什麼。

文法練習題

1. What really matters is not how much you read but _____ you read.
   - (A) also
   - (B) whether
   - (C) what
   - (D) for

2. Mr. Wang teaches you many things. He's not your enemy _____ your friend.
   - (A) or
   - (B) but
   - (C) and
   - (D) only

解答： **1. C   2. B**

翻譯練習題

1. 這不是你父母的責任而是你自己的。
2. 她愛你不是因為你很帥，而是因為你心地非常善良。

解答：

1. This is not your parents' responsibility but your own.
2. She loves you not because you are handsome but because you are a man with a heart of gold.

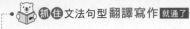

關鍵句型 8：not only...but also...

★ **not only A but (also) B**
不僅A，而且B【AB詞性要相等】

★ **Not only + 倒裝句, but + 主詞 + (also) + V**
→【倒裝方法：1. 助動詞＋S　2. be＋S
3. do/does/did＋S＋一般動詞】

例 Three years of constant training has made me <u>not only</u> more efficient <u>but (also)</u> more learned.
三年持續不斷的鍛鍊使我不但更有效率，而且也更有學問。

例 My teacher is serious <u>not only</u> to her own daughter <u>but (also)</u> to her students.
我的老師不單單對待她的女兒嚴格，對她的學生也是一樣。

例 <u>Not only</u> does my dog bark at the strangers to look after the house, <u>but it (also)</u> accompanies me when I feel lonely.
我的狗不僅對陌生人吠叫看家，也在我覺得寂寞時陪伴我。

例 <u>Not only</u> was she a popular singer, <u>but</u> she <u>also</u> excelled at composition.
她不但是一個流行歌手，而且也擅長作曲。

文法練習題

1. Dr. Ho prescribed not only medicine but also ＿＿＿＿＿ from the therapy dogs of his hospital.
   (A) have visits
   (B) visits
   (C) visited
   (D) to be visited

2. My home is a shelter, not only for my body ＿＿＿＿＿ for my mind.
   (A) but also
   (B) except
   (C) besides
   (D) as

3. Not only ＿＿＿＿＿＿＿ train individuals but it is also a vital factor for positive social change.
   (A) education
   (B) education does
   (C) does education
   (D) do education

解答： **1. B**　　**2. A**　　**3. C**

翻譯練習題

1. 她不但是第一流的設計家，而且也擅長插畫。
   (用Not only開頭)

2. 有了狗的存在，我的祖母不僅感覺更快樂，而且也更放鬆。

3. 幫助別人不但給我帶來友誼，也讓我覺得快樂。

解答:

1. Not only is she a first-rate designer, but she also excels at illustrations.

2. With the presence of dogs, my grandmother feels not only happier but (also) more relaxed.

3. Helping others not only brings me friendship but (also) makes me feel happy.

關鍵句型 9：主詞跟動詞的一致

(Both) A and B	複數動詞	A和B兩者都
Either A or B Niether A nor B Not only A but also B	動詞 【與主詞B一致】	不是A就是B A和B都不是 不僅僅是A，而且B也是
A but/except B A together with/along with B A as well as/no less than B	動詞 【與主詞A一致】	除了B之外 A跟B一起 A跟B一樣

例 (Both) Vicky and Joe like to play basketball.

維琪和喬兩人都喜歡打籃球。

例 Either you or your boss <u>has</u> to attend the meeting today.
你或是你的老闆今天必須去開會。

例 Neither my sister nor I <u>am</u> interested in singing English songs.
我姐姐跟我都對唱英文歌沒興趣。

例 Not only the employees but also the employer <u>looks</u> forward to the coming holidays.
不但員工期待即將到來的假日,老闆也是。

例 Nobody but my parents <u>knows</u> how to open the safe deposit box.
除了我父母之外,沒有人知道如何打開這個保險箱。

例 The vase together with the seeds <u>was</u> stolen.
花瓶連同種子一起被偷了。

例 Mark no less than his sons <u>is</u> handsome.
馬克和他的兒子們一樣的英俊。

文法練習題

1. Neither my husband nor my sons _____ interested in the film.
   (A) is
   (B) are

    (C) being

    (D) be

2. Vincent, along with his friends, _____ going for a trip next month.

    (A) is

    (B) are

    (C) being

    (D) be

解答：　**1. B**　　**2. A**

翻譯練習題

1. 我先生和他的同事曾去過紐約。
2. 不是你就是你老闆預期本周要做出決定。

解答：

1. My husband as well as his colleagues has been to New York.
2. Either you or your boss is due to make a decision this week.

關鍵句型 10：準關係代名詞代替整句

★ 句, which/as + 不完整句. 　**[which 或 as 都做「準關係代名詞」用，代替「前句」。]**
　= As + 不完整句, 句.

例 He is good at singing English songs, which everybody knows.

= He is good at singing English songs, as everybody knows.

= <u>As</u> everybody knows, he is good at singing English songs

大家都知道，他很會唱英文歌。

文法練習題

1. A library usually has air-conditioned rooms, ＿＿ makes it a pleasant place to stay.
   (A) hence
   (B) what
   (C) that
   (D) which

2. ＿＿ is known, the moon is closer to us than the sun.
   (A) Which
   (B) That
   (C) As
   (D) It

解答： 1. D　　2. C

翻譯練習題

1. 許多頑皮的小孩會在街道上玩球，這讓那個老先生很生氣。【用which代替整句】
2. 如同報紙所報導的，有三家銀行已經釋出意願要投資那家公司。【用as代替整句】

解答：

1. Many naughty children would play balls on the street, which made the old man very angry.

2. As has been reported by newspapers, three banks have expressed willingness to invest in that company.

= Three banks have expressed willingness to invest in that company, as has been reported by newspapers.

關鍵句型 11：what 所引導的名詞子句

【重點一】

what 複合關係 代名詞	= 先行詞 the N(s) +	關係代名詞 that/which

→[what 所引導的子句是名詞子句，可做 S/O/C]

例 Love is what the child needs.

= Love is the thing which the child needs.

= Love is the thing that the child needs.
愛是這個小孩所需要的東西。

例 What (= The thing which)(= The thing that) our manager really did was to improve the service quality.
我們經理真正做的事是去改善服務品質。

【重點二】what／all (that) + 不完整句 = 名詞
子句

例 Can you remember clearly <u>what</u> the
lecturer has said?

= Can you remember clearly <u>all that</u> the
lecturer has said?

= Can you remember clearly <u>all</u> the lecturer
has said?
那個講師所說的話你都記得清楚嗎？

【重點三】What + 不完整句 (含 do) + is + (to)
V

→某人能做的只有

→= All (that) + 不完整句 (含 do) + is + (to)
V

= The only thing (that) + 不完整句 (含
do) + is + (to) V

例 Now, what I can do is (to) apologize to you.

= Now, all (that) I can do is (to) apologize to
you.

= Now, the only thing (that) I can do is (to)
apologize to you.
現在我能做的就是跟你道歉。

文法練習題

1. _____ I'll do is leave a note for my mother to tell her I won't be back till the party is over.
   (A) What
   (B) It
   (C) That
   (D) Which

2. All I can do is _____ you for what you have done
   for my children.
   (A) thank
   (B) thanks
   (C) thanking
   (D) thankful

解答： 1. A　　2. A

翻譯練習題

1. 我要給你看看我買的東西。【用what引導的名詞子句】
2. 我不知道我父母親怎麼想的，但是如果你問他們，他們也許會給你一些建議。【用what引導的名詞子句】

解答：

1. I want to show you what I have bought.
2. I don't know what my parents think, but if you ask them, they might give you some suggestions.

關鍵句型 12：感嘆句型

How + 句！	
How + adj + S + be! **How + adv + S + V!**	多麼的…
How + adj + it + be + to V!	
How + adj + a N + (S + V/be)! **= What + N片 + (S + V/be)!**	

例 How I wish (that) I could pass the exam!
   我多麼希望可以通過考試阿！

例 How excited I am when I see her on the stage!
   當我看到她在舞台上，我是多麼的興奮阿！

例 How well she could speak English! I was so impressed.
   她英文說得多麼好啊！我真是印象深刻。

例 How embarrassing it is to buy a gift for your girlfriend without the money to pay for it!
   買禮物給女朋友卻沒錢付帳是多麼尷尬的事情阿！

例 How responsible a teacher (Miss Chen is)!
   = What a responsible teacher (Miss Chen is)!
   （陳老師是）多麼盡責的一個老師啊！

文法練習題

1. The lady petted the dog's head and said, "_____ a nice dog you are!"
   - (A) How
   - (B) What
   - (C) That
   - (D) It

2. Now, he can look with amusement at _____ funny he must have been when he was young.
   - (A) how
   - (B) what
   - (C) that
   - (D) it

解答： 1. B   2. A

翻譯練習題

1. 多麼尷尬的一次經驗啊！
2. 你怎麼有臉要求那樣的東西！

解答：

1. How embarrassing an experience it was!
   (= What an embarrassing experience it was!)
2. How you have the face to ask for such a thing!

關鍵句型 13：插入語句型

★此類插入語多數由以下動詞所組成：say, think, guess, believe, consider, imagine, suppose

★插入語的結構如下：

		say
		think
		guess
do	**you**	**believe**
		consider
		imagine
		suppose

★插入語放在以疑問詞為首的問句中，原疑問句的主詞與助動詞則不倒裝：

疑問詞	插入語		主詞與助動詞不倒裝	
What **How much** **How often** **When** **Who** **Where** **Why** **Which**	**do**	**say** **think** **guess** **believe** **consider** **imagine** **suppose**	+ (主詞)	+ 助動詞 + **V?** + 動詞?

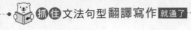

例 What do you think she will buy in this store?
你覺得她在這家店會買什麼？

例 When do you guess she will come to the party?
你猜她什麼時候會來派對？

例 Who do you believe would win the speech contest?
你認為誰會贏得演講比賽？

文法練習題

1. What _____ we all go to a restaurant downtown?
   (A) you say
   (B) say you
   (C) you do say
   (D) do you say

2. When do you suppose _____ arrive?
   (A) the rescue team
   (B) will the rescue team
   (C) the rescue team will
   (D) will

解答： 1. D   2. C

翻譯練習題

1. 你覺得我的錶值多少錢?
2. 你猜哪一個是員工離職最常見的理由?

解答:

1. How much do you think my watch is worth?

2. Which do you guess is the most common reason for an employee to quit?

五、認識常見動詞(片語)的用法

關鍵句型 1：感官動詞

【重點一】 sound/look/smell/taste/feel (感官 V) + adj
聽起來/看起來/聞起來/嚐起來/感到…

【重點二】 sound/look/smell/taste/feel (感官 V) + like (像) + N
聽起來像是/看起來像是/聞起來像是/嚐起來像是/感到像是…

【重點三】

感官動詞 hear/listen to/see/ watch/look at/notice/ smell/feel	O	V-ing [強調進行]
		V [強調事實]
		pp [表被動]

例 The idea sounds wonderful to me.
這主意對我來說聽起來很棒。

例 His new song sounds like rock music.
他的新歌聽起來像搖滾樂。

例 Can you hear someone knocking?
你聽到有人在敲門嗎？

例 The boy saw a dog run by.
這個男孩看見一隻狗跑過去。

例 John <u>saw the wounded policeman taken to</u> a nearby hospital.

約翰看到受傷的警察被送到附近的一家醫院。

文法練習題

1. Luna saw her husband _____ into the taxi last night.
   - (A) to get
   - (B) gets
   - (C) got
   - (D) get

2. The policeman noticed a man _____ on the ground.
   - (A) to lie
   - (B) lay
   - (C) lying
   - (D) lain

【提醒】lie (動詞) 躺。其動詞變化為 lie/lay/lain/lying

解答： 1. D 2. C

翻譯練習題

1. 我看到一輛車撞到這位老先生。我打電話給警方,然後看著他被送去醫院。

2. 昨天當我在公園散步時,我看到她的小孩在放風箏。

解答:

1. I saw a car hit the old man. I called the police and watched him taken to a hospital.

2. When I took a walk in the park yesterday, I saw her kids playing a kite.

關鍵句型 2:使役動詞

S	let	O	V	使、讓某受詞…
	make		adj V (表主動) pp (表被動)	
	have		adj V/V-ing (表主動) pp (表被動)	

例 The landlord finally agreed to let her stay.
最後房東終於同意讓她留下來。

例 It makes me so angry to see the stray dog being treated like that.
看到流浪狗受到那樣的對待我非常氣憤。

例 Mr. Wang's jokes made all his students laugh.
王老師的笑話把他所有的學生都逗笑了。

例 Miss Lin had to shout to make herself heard above the students' talking.
林老師不得不大聲喊叫以使學生們在說話聲中聽到她。

【提醒】使用**make**時，注意主、被動句型的替換寫法：

例 She made me wait two hours.
= I was made to wait two hours for her.
她讓我等了兩個小時。

例 Why don't you like to have the window open?
你為什麼不喜歡開著窗戶？

例 I'll have Linda show you to your office.
我會讓琳達帶你去看你的辦公室。

例 He had her secretary writing all kinds of letters for him.
他指使他的秘書替他寫各種各樣的信件。

例 The cook had his hands burned.
這個廚師把手給燙傷了。

文法練習題

1. Some teachers like to make their students
   _____ all day long. But it is not good.
   (A) studying
   (B) study
   (C) to study
   (D) studies

2. My mother finally _____ me buy a new
   computer.
   (A) wanted
   (B) told
   (C) let
   (D) asked

【提醒】**want/tell/ask + O + to + V**

3. David really loves playing basketball, but
   he can't play it now. He had his hands
   _____ last week.
   (A) hurt
   (B) hurting
   (C) hurts
   (D) hurtful

【提醒】**hurt (動詞) 受傷。三態同形:hurt/
hurt/hurt**

解答: 1. B 2. C 3. A

翻譯練習題

1. 茱蒂希望可以在家養貓,但她媽媽不讓她養。【用let】
2. 我想知道你通常在哪裡剪髮。【用have】
3. 我為父親的健康擔憂,但醫生所說的那些安慰話使我感覺好多了。【用make】

解答:

1. Judy hopes to keep a cat at home, but her mom doesn't let her do it.
2. I would like to know where you normally have your hair done.
3. I worried over my father's health, but the doctor's reassuring comments made me feel better.

關鍵句型 3:keep/leave

keep leave	O	OC	使…保持在…某狀態, 使…處於…某狀態

→[OC = 受詞補語 = adj / V-ing (表主動或令人感到…的)/ pp (表被動或感到…的)/介片]

例 The teacher kept the students quiet (adj).
這個老師讓學生們別作聲。

例 Never leave children alone (adj) in the swimming pool.
絕對不要讓小孩獨自在游泳池。

例 The girl kept her boyfriend waiting (V-ing) for a long time.
這個女孩讓她的男友等很久。

例 The noise kept me annoyed (pp).
噪音讓我很惱怒。

【提醒】annoy (動詞) 使生氣。這裡的
annoyed 為 pp 做形容詞用，意思為
「感到惱怒的」。

例 Miss Chen's authoritarian classroom climate leaves her students in awe.
陳老師嚴格管教的課堂氣氛令他的學生敬畏。

【提醒】in awe (介係詞片語) 敬畏地】

文法練習題

1. Don't leave your little kids _____ near water.
   (A) play
   (B) playing
   (C) played
   (D) to play

2. These wonderful toys can keep the kids
   _____ for a while.

(A) excite

(B) excited

(C) exciting

(D) excitement

解答: **1. B**　　**2. B**

翻譯練習題

1. 付了房租後他身無分文。
2. 把夾克穿上，這樣可以保暖。

解答:

1. Paying for the rent left him without a cent.
2. Put on your jacket. It'll keep you warm.

關鍵句型 4：use

use + 東西 + to + V = 東西 + be used to + V = 東西 + be used for + 　N/V-ing	【主動式】使用東西去 … 【被動式】東西被用來 …
人+ be/get + used to + V-ing	某人習慣於…
used to + V	過去曾經… (暗示現在不)

例 The superstar <u>uses</u> this special pen <u>to sign</u>.

= This special pen <u>is used to sign</u> by the superstar.

= This special pen <u>is used for</u> signature/ signing by the superstar.
   這個超級巨星使用這支特別的筆來簽名。

例 We <u>use</u> this classroom <u>to do</u> the experiment.

= This classroom <u>is used to do</u> the experiment by us.

= This classroom <u>is used for</u> the experiment. 或

This classroom <u>is used for doing</u> the experiment.

我們使用這間教室做實驗。

例 I <u>am used to taking</u> the MRT to school, and my mother <u>gets used to taking</u> a bus to work.

我習慣搭捷運上學,而我媽媽習慣搭公車上班。

例 I <u>used to play</u> basketball on Sundays, but now I only play the guitar.

以前每逢周日我都會打籃球,但是現在我只彈吉他。

例 She <u>used to be</u> a teacher, but she retired last year.

她以前是老師,但在去年退休了。

文法練習題

1. Vicky _____ a professional basketball player, but now she only watches basketball games.
   - (A) uses to be
   - (B) is used to being
   - (C) used to be
   - (D) has been

2. I _____ alone. I don't want to have any roommates.
   - (A) used to live
   - (B) was
   - (C) am used to living
   - (D) get used to live

解答: **1. C**　**2. C**

翻譯練習題

1. 這塊地會被用來種花。
2. 我以前常在週末去打籃球，但我現在只在家裡彈鋼琴。

解答:

1. This land will be used to plant flowers.
   (= This land will be used for planting flowers.)
2. I used to play basketball on weekends, but now I just play the piano at home.

關鍵句型 5：seem/appear，it looks/sounds like

【重點一】S (非it) + seem/appear + to V
　　　　或 (to be) adj

= It seems/appears + that 句

【重點二】There + seem/appear + to be...
　　似乎有…

例 She seems to know more about her boyfriend than anyone else.

= It seems that she knows more about her boyfriend than anyone else.
她似乎比任何人都更了解她的男友。

例 Mark seems very satisfied (adj) with the new car.

= It seems that Mark is very satisfied with the new car.
馬克對新車好像很滿意。

★但是當it表示前面所提過的單數名詞時，仍可接不定詞。

例 He bought the watch. It seemed/appeared to be very cheap.
他買了這支手錶，似乎很便宜。

例 There seems to be a problem with this app.
這個應用程式好像有問題。

【提醒】口語用法，事情看起來／聽起來似乎…，可用

「**It looks/sounds like** + **(that)** 句」

例 It looks like my boyfriend will invite my parents to lunch.

我男朋友好像會邀請我的父母去吃午餐。

例 It sounds like he doesn't know what he is doing.

他好像不知道他在做什麼。

文法練習題

1. Lisa's words appeared to _____ her husband. He looked so angry.
   - (A) offend
   - (B) offending
   - (C) offense
   - (D) offended

2. They seem very _____ by the voice of the singer.
   - (A) fascinate
   - (B) fascinated
   - (C) fascinating
   - (D) fascination

解答： **1. A**   **2. B**

翻譯練習題

1. 這兩組在測試中似乎有很大的差異。
2. 他好像已經修改了計劃。

解答：

1. There appeared to be a great difference between the two groups in the test.
2. It seems that he has changed his plan.
   (= He seems to have changed his plan.)

關鍵句型 6：consider/think

【重點一】 consider/think + O + (to be) + N/adj

= consider/think + that句

= regard/think of/view/see/take + O + as + N/adj

【認為A是B】

【重點二】主被動的替換：

★ consider/think + A + (to be) + B (N/adj)

= A + be + considered/thought + (to be) + B (N/adj)

★ regard/think of/view/see/take + A + as + B (N/adj)

= A + be + regarded/thought of/viewed/seen/taken + as B (N/adj)

例 Some students don't <u>consider it (to be) wrong</u> to cheat in examinations.

= Some students don't <u>regard it as wrong</u> to cheat in examinations.

= Some students don't <u>consider (that) it is wrong</u> to cheat in examinations.

有些學生不認為考試作弊是錯誤的。

例 I <u>think it my duty</u> to take care of the pets.

= I <u>think (that)</u> it is my duty to take care of the pets.

= <u>It is thought (to be) my duty</u> to take care of the pets.

= I <u>regard it as my duty</u> to take care of the pets.

= <u>It is regarded as my duty</u> to take care of the pets.

我認為照顧這些寵物是我的職責。

【提醒】這裡的 it = to take care of the pets

文法練習題

1. Miss Lin considered Tom's words _____; she wanted to report it to his parents.
   (A) forgive
   (B) forgiveness
   (C) forgivable
   (D) unforgivable

2. My husband ＿＿＿＿ an honest man, or at least he never tells lies to me.
   (A) regards as
   (B) is regarded as
   (C) considers
   (D) is regarded

解答： 1. D 2. B

翻譯練習題

1. 你認為一個老師以這種方式去處罰一個學生是正確的嗎？【用 think】
2. 王老師，不要還把我看作小孩子。【用 think of】

解答：

1. Do you think it right for a teacher to punish a student in this way? (= Do you think (that) it is right for a teacher to punish a student in this way?)
2. Don't think of me as still a little child, Mr. Wang.

關鍵句型 7：find

【重點一】find + O + OC
→[OC = 受詞補語 = N／V-ing／pp／adj／介片]

【重點二】find + that句

例 They will find it <u>an interesting book</u>.
他們會發現它是本有趣的書。

例 I found the man <u>lying</u> on the ground.
我發現這個男人躺在地板上。

例 The police found the thief <u>caught</u> by the strong man.
警方發現這個小偷被這個強壯的男人逮住。

例 Did he find the job <u>boring</u>?
他發現這份工作無聊了嗎?

例 When he got back, he found a letter <u>on his desk</u>.
當他回家時,他發現書桌上有封信。

例 My husband woke to <u>find (that)</u> his quilt had slipped off the sofa.
我先生醒來發現被子從沙發上滑下來了。

文法練習題

1. He is in the habit of putting off till some future time what he should do today. Therefore, he often finds himself _____ what should have been finished earlier.

   (A) do
   (B) does
   (C) done
   (D) doing

2. I found the dog _____ on the sofa and
   the cat _____ under the piano.
   (A) sleep/wake
   (B) asleep/wake
   (C) asleep/awake
   (D) slept/awake

【提醒】 asleep (形容詞)睡著的；
        awake (形容詞)醒著的

解答： 　1. D　　2. C

翻譯練習題

1. 一旦你的先生染上壞習慣，想改掉就難
   了。
2. 隨著冬天的到來，要減肥更不容易了。

解答：

1. Once your husband gets into a bad habit,
   he'll find it hard to get out of it.
   (= Once your husband gets into a bad
   habit, he'll find (that) it is hard to get out
   of it.)

2. With the winter coming, I find it more
   difficult to lose weight.
= (With the winter coming, I find (that) it
   is more difficult to lose weight.)

關鍵句型 8：prefer

★ **prefer** + **N/Ving** + **to** + **N/Ving**

= **prefer to** + **V** + **rather than** + **V**

= **would rather** + **V** + **than** + **V**

= **had rather** + **V** + **than** + **V**

【寧可…也不願…】

例 The child <u>prefers</u> going out <u>to</u> staying at home.

= The child <u>prefers to</u> go out <u>rather than</u> stay at home.

= The child <u>would rather</u> go out <u>than</u> stay at home.

= The child <u>had rather</u> go out <u>than</u> stay at home.

這孩子寧可出去也不願待在家裡。

文法練習題

1. I would rather _____ silent than _____ to him.
   - (A) keep/talk
   - (B) keeping/talking
   - (C) keep/talking
   - (D) keeping/talk

2. Mary hopes to live a simple life. She prefers a small country _____ a big city.
   - (A) than

(B) rather than

(C) as

(D) to

解答:　**1. A**　　**2. D**

翻譯練習題

1. 我寧可去，也不願留著被罵。【用 prefer to】
2. 他們寧可強調品質，而不願提升數量。【用 would rather】

解答:

1. I prefer to go rather than stay to be blamed.
2. They would rather emphasize quality than promote quantity.

關鍵句型 9：stop/remember/forget

【提醒】不定詞表「未來動作」，而動名詞表「過去經驗」，根據此原則，可判斷這三個動詞後面要接的是「不定詞」(to + V)，抑或是「動名詞」(V-ing)。

【重點一】

stop	to V	停下來去做另一件事 (在停止時，另一動作尚未做)
	V-ing	停止做 (在停止時，該動作已做過)

【重點二】

| remember | to V | 記得要去做 (記得尚未做的動作) |
| | V-ing | 記得曾做過 (記得已經做過的動作) |

【重點三】

| forget | to V | 忘記要去做 (忘記尚未做的動作) |
| | V-ing | 忘記曾做過 (忘記曾經做過的動作) |

例 On the way to the post office, John stopped to chat with Mary, and forgot to send his letter.

在去郵局的路上，約翰停下來跟瑪麗聊天，而忘了去寄信。

例 Didn't you receive my e-mail? I remember sending it two days ago.

你沒有收到我的電子郵件嗎？ 記得兩天前就寄出了。

文法練習題

1. I remember _____ the office about two hours ago.
   (A) to see her leave
   (B) to see her to leave
   (C) to see her leaving
   (D) seeing her leave

2. It's time for the math test. Please stop

    ____.

  (A) talk

  (B) to talk

  (C) talking

  (D) being talked

解答：   **1. D**   **2. C**

翻譯練習題

1.「你有記得帶護照嗎？」「哦，對不起，我忘了。」

2. 為了健康著想，他下定決心要戒菸。

解答：

1. "Did you remember to bring your passport?" "Oh, sorry, I forgot."

2. For the sake of health, he made up his mind to stop smoking.

關鍵句型 10：表建議，要求，主張等動詞

建議類 **propose, suggest, recommend, move**	+	that + 句 [= 主詞 + (should) + V] ★ should (助動詞) 應該【可省略，後接原形動詞】
要求類 **request, require, ask, demand, order, provide** (規定), **command** (命令)		
主張類 **insist, urge** (極力主張)		

例 He suggested that the meeting (should) be continued after lunch.
他建議午餐後繼續開會。

例 The manager required that I (should) work all night.
經理要求我通宵工作。

例 My best friend urged that I (should) quit the job.
我最好的朋友力勸我辭掉那份工作。

文法練習題

1. He asks that he ____ more time to complete the test.
   (A) gives
   (B) is given
   (C) be given
   (D) will be given

2. The chairman moved that the meeting ____ after lunch.
   (A) continues
   (B) continued
   (C) be continued
   (D) continuing

解答： 1. C 2. C

翻譯練習題

1. 這個情況非常棘手。我建議你找律師。
   【用 recommend】
2. 我的歌喉很差。我的老師建議我去上唱歌班。
   【用 suggest】

解答：

1. This situation is very tricky. I recommend that you (should) find a lawyer.
2. I have a bad voice. My teacher suggested that I (should) take a singing class.

關鍵句型 11：表花費等動詞

【重點一】事情 (非 it) + take (vt.需要) + 時間/抽象 N

　= it + takes + 時間/抽象 N + to V

　【某件事需要…】

例 The meeting will take three hours.
　會議要進行三小時。

例 It takes practice and time to play the guitar well.
　要彈好吉他需要練習和時間。

【重點二】人 + spend + 時間/金錢 + on N／(in) V-ing

　　　　　【人花費時間/金錢在…】

例 I spent 200 dollars on the book.
我花了兩百元買下那本書。

例 The young couple spent two months touring Europe.
那對年輕夫婦花了兩個月時間周遊歐洲。

【重點三】事/物 (非it) + cost + 人 + 錢
= it cost 人 + 錢 + to V
【某事/物花了某人多少錢】

【提醒】cost三態同形

例 The new house cost him a lot of money.
= It cost him a lot of money to buy the new house.
這棟新房子花費他很多錢。

例 That dress cost her six hundred dollars
= It cost her six hundred dollars to buy that dress.
她花了六百元買那件洋裝。

文法練習題

1. Organizing a successful meeting _____ a lot of time and money.
   (A) costs
   (B) spends
   (C) takes
   (D) makes

2. If you go to Taipei, you can _____ a whole night wandering around Shilin Night Market.
   (A) cost
   (B) spend
   (C) take
   (D) make

解答： **1. C**　　**2. B**

翻譯練習題

1. 她花了一年時間寫完這本書。【用 It took...】
2. 他花了五千塊買那隻手錶。【用 It cost...】

解答：

1. It took her a year to finish writing the book.
2. It cost him five thousand dollars to buy that watch.

關鍵句型 12：表致力、奉獻的動詞（片語）

【重點一】devote/dedicate + O + to + N/V-ing
　　　　　奉獻…在…；投注在…

【重點二】S + be devoted/dedicated to + N/V-ing 致力於…

【重點三】S + be engaged in + N/V-ing
　　　　　忙於、埋頭致力於…

= S + engage in + N/V-ing

[= S + work on + N

= S + be busy with + N]

例 He has devoted his whole life to protecting wild birds.
他一生致力於保護野生鳥類。

例 She was dedicated to a life of teaching, which gained the respect of her colleagues.
她獻身於教學事業,贏得了同事們的尊敬。

例 He has been engaged in writing a new song for the whole morning.

= He has engaged in writing a new song for the whole morning.

= He has worked on a new song for the whole morning.

= He has been busy with a new song for the whole morning.
他整個早上都在忙著寫新歌。

文法練習題

1. My parents _____ a discussion that might make some change for the better.

   (A) engage

   (B) are engaged

(C) engaging in

(D) are engaged in

2. _____ religious movements, people develop their moral spirit.

(A) Devote to

(B) Being devoted

(C) Devotion to

(D) Being devoted to

解答： 1. D 2. D

翻譯練習題

1. 整個晚上他們把全副精力投入這項任務。

【用 devote/dedicate + O + to + N】

2. 最近兩年她的時間都花在寫一本有關環保的書上。

【用 work on】

解答：

1. They devoted/dedicated all their energies to the task all night.

2. She has spent the last two years working on a book about environmental protection.

關鍵句型 13：表努力、盡力的動詞（片語）

【重點一】 make an effort to + V = exert oneself to + V 努力去

【重點二】spare no effort(s) + to V /in V-ing
　　　　盡力去

【重點三】do/try one's best to + V　盡其所能去

例 I have a date tonight. I will <u>make an effort</u>
<u>to</u> finish my work early.

= I have a date tonight. I will <u>exert myself</u>
<u>to</u> finish my work early.
我晚上有約會。我會努力提早完成工作。

例 The police are determined to <u>spare no effort</u>
<u>to</u> crack down on fraud rings.

= The police are determined to <u>spare no effort</u>
<u>in</u> cracking down on fraud rings.
警方決心要盡力打擊詐騙集團。

例 He felt so ill at ease that all he could do
was (to) stand there and <u>try his best to</u>
smile.
他感到那麼不自在，只能站在那裡盡力地
微笑。

文法練習題

1. This program allowed me to exert myself
   to ＿＿ much more than what was defined
   in the curriculum.
   (A) accomplish
   (B) accomplishing
   (C) accomplishment
   (D) being accomplished

2. The government has spared no effort
   _____ those whose homes were destroyed
   by the tornadoes.
   (A) help
   (B) helping
   (C) to help
   (D) helpful

解答：　1. A　　2. C

翻譯練習題

1. 里長極力主張大家都盡力讓環境保持乾
   淨。
   【用 make an effort...】
2. 教育部推動成人教育不遺餘力。
   【用 spare no efforts...】

解答：

1. The neighborhood manager urged that we
   all make an effort to keep our environment clean.
2. The Education Department has spared no
   efforts in promoting adult education.
   (= The Education Department has spared
   no efforts to promote adult education.)

關鍵句型 14：決定類動詞（片語）

★ **make the/人's decision to + V** 下定決心去 …

= **make up 人's mind to + V**

= **decide to + V** = **be decided to + V**

= **determine to + V** = **be determined to + V**

= **resolve to + V** = **be resolved to + V**

例 Even if it will take me a year, I have <u>made the decision to</u> finish writing the novel.

= Even if it will take me a year, I have <u>made up my mind to</u> finish writing the novel.

= Even if it will take me a year, I have <u>decided/ determined/resolved to</u> finish writing the novel.

= Even if it will take me a year, I have been <u>decided/determined/resolved to</u> finish writing the novel.

即使將花費一年的時間，我已決定要把這本小說寫完。

文法練習題

1. Every time he makes the decision ____ someone, he opens himself to great suffering.
   - (A) love
   - (B) to love
   - (C) loving
   - (D) being loved

2. At a very early age she made up her mind ____ an artist.
   - (A) become
   - (B) becoming
   - (C) became
   - (D) to become

解答: **1. B**　　**2. D**

翻譯練習題

1. 麗莎決定辭掉工作去追求兒時的夢想。
   【用 decide，過去式】
2. 他們決定至少每年視察我們的工廠一次。
   【用 resolve，過去式】

解答:

1. Lisa (was) decided to quit her job to pursue her childhood dream.
2. They (were) resolved to visit our factory at least once a year.

關鍵句型 15：成功、失敗類動詞（片語）

★ **fail to + V** 失敗；未能去…

★ **never fail to + V** 總是會…

★ **succeed in + N/V-ing** 成功；順利完成…

★ **only succeed + in N/V-ing** 取得相反的效果；弄巧成拙

例 He did a very good job, but <u>failed to keep</u> his promise.
他表現得很出色，但未能信守承諾。

例 My best friend Luna <u>never fails to give</u> me a gift on my birthday.
我最好的朋友露娜總會在我生日時送我禮物。

例 The negotiators between the two countries have not yet <u>succeeded in reaching</u> a conclusion.
兩國之間的談判者仍未達成結論。

例 You've talked too much and <u>only succeeded in upsetting</u> your guest.
你說太多了，這樣反而弄得你的客人不高興了。

文法練習題

1. He is a good magician. He never fails
   ____ me.
   (A) surprise
   (B) surprising
   (C) to surprise
   (D) being surprised

2. We need to plan everything very carefully
   to succeed ____ this enterprise.
   (A) in
   (B) on
   (C) of
   (D) to

解答: 1. C 2. A

翻譯練習題

1. 有些人無法接受自己原本的模樣而想成
   為其他人。
2. 只要我繼續努力,我就能達成我的理想。

解答:

1. Some people fail to accept what they are
   and want to be someone else.
2. As long as I keep on working hard, I
   will succeed in reaching my ideal.

關鍵句型 16：爆裂、突然類動詞片語

★ burst vi. 爆裂；突然發生 (三態同形)

→**burst/break + into tears** 突然大哭

[= burst out crying]

→**burst/break + into laughter** 突然大笑

[= burst out laughing]

例 On hearing the bad news, she burst into tears.

= On hearing the bad news, she broke into tears.

= On hearing the bad news, she burst out crying.

= On hearing the bad news, she cried loudly all of a sudden.

聽到這個壞消息，她突然大哭。

例 Only when the clown came on stage would the audience burst into laughter.

= Only when the clown came on stage would the audience break into laughter.

= Only when the clown came on stage would the audience burst out laughing.

= Only when the clown came on stage would the audience laugh loudly all of a sudden.

只有當那個小丑上台時，觀眾才會突然大笑。

文法練習題

1. When the earthquake happened last night, the little child cried ____ all of a sudden.
   - (A) tears
   - (B) into laughter
   - (C) tearing
   - (D) loudly

2. If the joke is funny enough, I might
   ____.
   - (A) burst into laughter
   - (B) burst out tears
   - (C) bump into laughing
   - (D) break into something

解答： 1. D 2. A

翻譯練習題

1. 當她收到這早來的洋娃娃聖誕節禮物時，她突然大哭。【用 burst into】
2. 我覺得她很情緒化。她常常沒有理由的突然大哭。
   【用 burst out】

解答：

1. She burst into tears when she received the early Christmas gift of a doll.
2. I think she is very emotional. She often bursts out crying
   for no apparent reason.

關鍵句型 17：遇見、撞見類動詞片語

★ run into	
= run across	
= bump into	
= come across	偶遇、撞見
= come upon	
= fall in with	
= meet with	
★ run across	
= come across	意外找到

例 I had no idea he was in the office. I just <u>ran into</u> him accidentally there.
我並不知道他在辦公室，只是無意中在那裡碰見了他。

例 How amazing it is to <u>run across</u> one of her earliest CDs in a second-hand shop!
在一個二手商店裡意外地找到了她早期的一個CD，真是令人驚奇！

文法練習題

1. If you ___ any spelling mistakes in reviewing my composition, please correct them for me.
   (A) burst into
   (B) look into

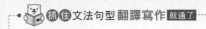

(C) come across

(D) get into

2. Don't wear shorts and slippers. You often _____ your friends at the grocery store.

(A) look down upon

(B) break into

(C) burst into

(D) bump into

解答： 1. C　2. D

翻譯練習題

1. 昨天我無意中找到一張舊照片，喚起了一些回憶。
   【用 run across】
2. 我真的很高興昨天我們在餐廳不期而遇。
   【用 run into】

解答：

1. I ran across an old picture yesterday. It brought back memories.
2. I'm really glad that we ran into each other at the restaurant yesterday.

關鍵句型 18：想到、想出類動詞片語

★ think up = come up with = think of	想出
★ think of	想到，打算
★ think about	想起；考慮
★ think back + on/to	回想起、回頭看

【補充句型】it occurs to 人 + that 句　某人想起、想到

例 My girlfriend's birthday is coming soon. Can you come up with a good place for her birthday party?
我女友的生日就快要到了。你能想出一個好地方來辦她的生日派對嗎？

例 Don't be so selfish. We must think of other people.
不要這麼自私。我們要替別人設想。

例 It's probably going to rain tomorrow. We are thinking of cancelling the game.
明天可能會下雨。我們打算取消比賽。

例 Every time they think about the endangered species of birds, they blame the government.
每當他們想起瀕臨絕種的鳥類，他們就譴責政府。

例 I hope to <u>think about</u> my future plan before I give a definite answer.

= I hope to <u>reflect on</u> my future plan before I give a definite answer.

我希望先考慮一下我的未來計劃，才能做出明確的答覆。

例 When he <u>thinks back on</u> it, he is not sure whether it was a wrong choice or not.

當他回頭看這件事，他無法確定那是否是個錯誤的選擇。

例 <u>It</u> never <u>occurred to me that</u> I might win the grand prize.

我怎麼也沒想到我會贏得大獎。

文法練習題

1. I _____ Mark immediately when they said they wanted someone who can play the guitar.
   - (A) looked up to
   - (B) ran after
   - (C) thought of
   - (D) fooled around

2. When I _____ my days as a guitar player, I smile broadly.
   - (A) come across
   - (B) come up with
   - (C) look down upon

(D) think back on

解答： 1. C 　 2. D

翻譯練習題

1. 我們的行銷人員已經想出替新產品促銷的好點子。
   【用come up with】
2. 中學階段是我開始會去考慮自己的生活和目標的時候。 【用think about】

解答：

1. Our marketing people have come up with a great idea for promoting the new product.
2. The high school period is a time when I begin to think about my life and goals.

關鍵句型 19：強調、著重類動詞（片語）

★ emphasize
  = put/lay + emphasis/stress + on
  = lay weight on
  = highlight
  = stress

★ emphasize + that句
  = It is emphasized + that句.

例 The mayor made a speech to emphasize the need for environmental protection.

= To put stress on the need for environmental protection, the mayor made a speech.
  市長發表了演講來強調環保的需要性。

例 Mr. Chen emphasized (that) every student should come on time.

= It was emphasized by Mr. Chen that every student should come on time.

陳老師強調每個學生都應該準時到。

文法練習題

1. One's appearance can't represent anything. We had better _____ his inner merits.
   - (A) rely on
   - (B) put on
   - (C) crack down on
   - (D) put emphasis on

2. In the international forum, Dr. Ho stressed the importance of mathematics to the whole of science. (選出同義字)
   - (A) highlighted
   - (B) ignored
   - (C) imported
   - (D) enhanced

解答： **1. D** **2. A**

翻譯練習題

1. 我的老闆總是強調這份工作在效率上的重要性。
   【用 lay stress on】

2. 這個學者逐漸傾向於強調那些士兵任務的艱鉅,並給予同情。【用 lay weight on】

解答:

1. My boss always lays stress on the importance of efficiency in this job.

2. The scholar became more and more inclined to lay weight on the difficulties of the soldiers' task and sympathized with them.

關鍵句型 20:影響類動詞(片語)

★ **have/make + a + adj + influence/impact/effect + on** 對象
   【對某對象有…的影響】

★ **A + affect/influence + B** 【A影響B】
   = **B + be affected/influenced by + A** 【B 被A影響】

例 His father lost his job. This might <u>have a great inpact on</u> him.
   他爸爸失業了。這也許會對他影響很大。

例 Classical music afftected this singer's music much.

= This singer's music was much influenced by classical music.

這個歌手的音樂深受古典樂的影響。

文法練習題

1. Without goals in our life, we will be influenced by
   others and go astray easily. (選同義字)
   (A) affected
   (B) effected
   (C) escaped
   (D) aroused

2. Parental influence can be a major factor in reducing the _____ that television violence will have on children.
   (A) affect
   (B) impact
   (C) revolt
   (D) instinct

解答： 1. A　　2. B

翻譯練習題

1. 這本書很暢銷，對讀者有很大的影響。
   【用 have a...influence on】
2. 先生癌症的病情使她深受影響。
   【用 affect】

解答：

1. This book sold well, and it had a great influence on its readers.
2. The state of her husband's cancer affected her deeply.
= She was deeply affected by the state of her husband's cancer.

關鍵句型 21：關心、關係類動詞 (片語)

be concerned with	跟…有關
be concerned with/about (= care about)	對…關心
care for (= take care of)	對…照顧
attend (to) look after	關心、照料、護理
as far as 對象 be concerned	就…而言
the authorities concerned	有關當局

例 This story is concerned with a single parent family in a big city.

這個故事寫的是大都市的一個單親家庭。

例 If you care about him, you should talk to him about his problems.
如果你關心他，你應該跟他聊聊他的問題。

例 How can you expect her not to be concerned about her son's school performance?
你怎麼會要她不去關心自己兒子的在校表現呢？

例 As far as I am concerned, what my parents said is important.
就我而言，父母親說的話是重要的。

例 The authorities concerned should deal with noise pollution in our community as soon as possible.
有關當局應該盡快處理我們社區的噪音。

文法練習題

1. Who will _____ your cat while you are away?
   (A) intend
   (B) look for
   (C) take care
   (D) care for

2. The politician seems to be far more concerned with getting elected than with passing legislation.

(A) 關心

(B) 照料

(C) 關於

(D) 打算

解答： 1. D 2. A

翻譯練習題

1. 麗莎對她的同事如何看待自己從來不太在意。

【用 be concerned about】

2. 這些信主要是關於面試邀請的範例。

【用 be concerned with】

解答：

1. Lisa has never been particularly concerned about what her colleagues think of her.

2. These letters are chiefly concerned with examples of interview invitations.

關鍵句型 22：參加類動詞 (片語)

take part in = participate in = join in	+ 活動	參加…活動
join	+ 團體	參入…團體

例 I like to play the guitar. I join a guitar club to practice playing the guitar with the club's members every Thursday night.

我喜歡彈吉他。我加入一個吉他社每周四晚上跟社員一起練習彈吉他。

例 He opened a new shop last week. Did you <u>take part in</u> the opening ceremony of his new shop?

上周他開了一家新店。你有參加他新店的開幕典禮嗎？

文法練習題

1. Everyone in my class is expected to ___ ___ in this activity.

(A) participate

(B) present

(C) donate

(D) dodge

2. Lisa _____ the Daily News as a reporter in 1996.

(A) participated

(B) involved

(C) joined

(D) confounded

解答： **1. A**　　**2. C**

翻譯練習題

1. 讓學生參與課堂討論是重要的。
   【用 participate in】
2. 我們想要邀請你參加這周五下午的會議。
   【用 join in】

解答:

1. It is important to get students to participate in classroom discussions.
2. We would like to invite you to join in a meeting in this Friday afternoon.

關鍵句型 23:組成類動詞(片語)

組成份子	compose constitute make up	全體	全體由…所組成,全體包含了…組成分子
全體	be made up of be composed/comprised of contain comprise consist of	組成份子	

例 Our guitar club is composed of one teacher and ten students.
我們的吉他社由一個老師及十個學生所組成。

例 The book consists of a large number of different articles and illustrations.
這本書由許多文章及插圖所組成。

例 Taiwanese people <u>make up</u> over 80% of this city's population.

這座城市超過八成的人口由台灣人所組成。

文法練習題

1. The band <u>is comprised of</u> a guitarist, a bassist, and
   a drummer.
   - (A) gets rid of
   - (B) is deprived of
   - (C) makes up
   - (D) consists of

2. This CD _____ many old songs from the 1960s.
   - (A) contains
   - (B) composes
   - (C) resembles
   - (D) withdraws

解答: 1. D　　2. A

翻譯練習題

1. 這座房子有一間臥室、一間廚房、一間客廳跟一間浴室。【用comprise】
2. 今天的晚餐有一道開胃菜、一道主菜和一個甜點。
   【用consist of】

解答：

1. The house comprises a bedroom, a kitchen, a living room, and a bathroom. (= The house is comprised of a bedroom, a kitchen, a living room, and a bathroom.)
2. Tonight's dinner consisted of a starter, a main course and a dessert.

關鍵句型 24：原因類動詞 (片語)

【重點一】

因	cause	果
	lead to	
	result in	
	bring about	
	give rise to	
★ cause + O + to + V		

【重點二】

果	be caused by	因
	be attributed to	
	arise from	
	result from	
★ attribute + 果 + to + 因		

例 A childhood illness <u>caused</u> her difficulty in running.

= A childhood illness <u>led to</u> her difficulty in running.

= A childhood illness <u>resulted in</u> her difficulty in running.

= A childhood illness <u>brought about</u> her difficulty in running.

= A childhood illness <u>gave rise to</u> her difficulty in running.
　幼時生病造成她跑步困難。

例 He <u>attributed</u> his success <u>to</u> diligence.

= His success <u>was attributed</u> to diligence.

= His success <u>was caused by</u> diligence.

= His success <u>arose from</u> diligence.

= His success <u>resulted from</u> diligence.
　他認為自己之所以成功是因為勤奮。

例 A cat ran into the road, <u>causing</u> the motorist to stop his car.
　一隻貓跑到了道路上，使得那位駕駛者將車停了下來。

文法練習題

1. Most road accidents <u>are caused by</u> human error.
   (A) are related to
   (B) result in

(C) bring about

(D) arise from

2. The entrepreneur attributes his success
   _____ his wife's support.

   (A) from

   (B) to

   (C) off

   (D) for

解答： **1. D**　**2. B**

翻譯練習題

1. 緊張和疲勞常導致缺乏效率。【用result in】
2. 這個研究發現一些在運動競賽中成功的要素。
   【用lead to】

解答：

1. Stress and tiredness often result in lack of efficiency.
2. The study found some key factors leading to success in sports games.

關鍵句型 25：「vt + that句」，「vt + 人+ that句」，「vt + to 人+ that句」

【重點一】常見的「vt + that句」

　→[此句型中的 that 句為名詞子句，作

為及物動詞 (vt) 的受詞 (O)。如是第
一個 that 句,則 that 可以 省略。]

vt (及物動詞)		中文意思
say		說…
mention		提到…
comment		評論…
hope		希望…
believe		相信…
think/consider		想,認為…
feel		覺得…
hear		聽說…
find/discover		發現…
notice/observe		看到,注意到…
know		知道…
realize	+ that 句	了解到…
show/indicate		顯示…
imagine		想像…
expect		期待…
beg		請求…
remember		記得…
mention		提到…
mean		意指…
dictate		規定…
explain		解釋…
complain		抱怨…
guess		猜測…
swear		發誓、保證…

【提醒】兩個或多個that所引導的名詞子句,
　　　　當同一個vt的受詞時,只有第一個
　　　　that可以省略,其他不可省略。

例 She said (that) she had been better and that she had forgiven him. However, we could not help feeling worried about her.
她說她已經好多了,也已經原諒他,不過我們還是忍不住擔心她。

例 I thought (that) he was single. He never mentioned (that) he had been married.
我以為他單身。他從沒提起已婚。

例 Some critics have commented (that) the film is a pioneering work, and they believe (that) it will go down in history.
一些評論家評述這部電影是個創舉,而且他們相信這部電影會被記載在歷史上。

例 We consider (that) he gambles heavily on the stock exchange. We can't imagine (that) he loses all his money on it.
我們認為他在股票交易上下了大賭注。我們無法想像他因為這樣輸光了所有錢。

例 I know (that) he has a very hard life. I feel (that) he is getting less energetic.
我知道他日子過得很艱難。我覺得他越來越沒有活力。

例 This coffee club rules dictated (that) their members must wear suitable footwear, so I didn't expect (that) you'd wear slippers.
這個咖啡俱樂部的規定要求他們的會員必須穿著適當的鞋子,所以我沒料到你會穿拖鞋。

例 Many research reports have shown (that) passive smoking does harm to our health.
很多研究報告已經顯示二手煙對我們的健康有害。

例 My grandmother has discovered (that) petting a dog can lower her blood pressure.
我的祖母已經發現撫摸狗兒可以降低她的血壓。

例 Memorizing the dialogues in the text does not mean (that) you are able to communicate with foreigners in English.
會背課本上的對話，並不表示你可以用英文跟外國人溝通。

例 I suddenly remembered (that) I hadn't locked the door, so I rushed back home.
我突然想起來我沒有鎖門，所以我衝回家。

例 He was shocked to hear (that) he had failed in the exam. He begged (that) neither of you would say anything.
聽到考試沒通過，他很震驚。他求你們誰也別說了。

例 Your husband realizes now (that) you mean more to him than anything else.
妳的先生現在了解你對他比其他任何東西更重要。

【重點二】常見的「vt + 人 + that句」，「vt + to 人 + that句」

tell	人	+ that 句	告訴某人…
warn			警告某人…
say	to 人		對某人說…
explain			對某人解釋…
complain			對某人抱怨…

例 I told my boss that when I got to the station the client had already gone.

我告訴我的老闆當我到車站的時候客戶已經走了。

例 We warned them that a typhoon was coming.

我們警告他們颱風快來了。

例 One day, my mother said to me that she felt proud of my good performance in music.

有一天，我媽媽跟我說她對我在音樂方面的優異表現感到驕傲。

例 The boy was frightened, but I explained to him that it was just a game.

這個男孩嚇到了，但我還是跟他解釋說這只是遊戲。

文法練習題

1. Mr. Lin _____ to me that you hadn't been to school for the last few days; I think I had better call your parents.
   (A) told
   (B) said
   (C) occurred
   (D) happened

2. He _____ that the exam was too hard. He studied hard but still failed.
   (A) expected
   (B) warned
   (C) complained
   (D) behaved

3. We had a great meal tonight. I never _____ that you might be hungry at midnight.
   (A) explained
   (B) intrigued
   (C) improved
   (D) thought

解答： 1. B　　2. C　　3. D

翻譯練習題

1. 我不是想要跟你們一起吃晚餐。我想我是沒說清楚。【用 mean, guess】
2. 我從未想過我能做到,但我辦到了。【用 think】
3. 她告訴男友說她不是被他的外表而是被他邪惡的心所嚇到。

解答:

1. I didn't mean (that) I wanted to join you for dinner. I guess (that) I haven't explained myself very well.
2. I never thought (that) I could do it, but I made it.
3. She told her boyfriend (that) she was horrified not by his appearance but by his evil heart.

關鍵句型 26：vt + V-ing

→本句型中的 V-ing 為「動名詞」，作為 vt (及物動詞) 的受詞 (O)。常見的如下表：

vt (及物動詞)		中文意思
admit		承認…
avoid		避免…
cease		停止…
consider		考慮…
continue		繼續…
delay		耽擱…
deny		否認…
dread		害怕…
enjoy		享受…
endure		忍受…
escape		逃過，免於…
evade		逃避
finish		完成…
hate	+ V-ing	討厭…
imagine		想像…
include		包括
intend		打算…
involve		包含，涉及…
keep		保持…
like/love		喜歡，喜愛…
mind		介意…
postpone		耽擱，延遲…
practice		練習…
prefer		較喜歡…
quit		放棄，戒除…
risk		冒著…的風險
stop		停止…
suggest		建議…

例 She <u>kept telling</u> a story to her children without seeing that they were sleepy.
她一直說故事給她的小孩聽,而沒有注意到他們已經想睡了。

例 The doctor suggested that I (should) keep early hours and <u>avoid staying</u> up doing anything.
醫生建議我早睡早起,並避免熬夜做任何事情。

例 She's <u>considering studying</u> abroad. That's why she <u>postponed accepting</u> his marriage proposal.
她正考慮要出國念書。那就是她遲遲沒有接受他求婚的原因。

例 She <u>denied having</u> an affair with her boss that had lasted for two years.
她否認跟她的老闆有兩年的曖昧關係。

【注意】下列二個動詞片語,後面也是加「動名詞 (V-ing)」

1. end up + Ving/介片 最後…

例 At first he tried to make excuses but he <u>ended up apologizing</u>.
最初他試著找藉口,到頭來還是道了歉。

2. feel like + N/Ving 想要

例 She doesn't want tea. She <u>feels like having</u> a cup of coffee.
她不想喝茶。她想要來杯咖啡。

文法練習題

1. My mother was in a good mood. We were lucky to escape ____.
   - (A) punish
   - (B) punished
   - (C) punishing
   - (D) being punished

2. We will be on holiday for a week. Would you mind ____ care of our dog?
   - (A) take
   - (B) to take
   - (C) taking
   - (D) taken

解答： 1. D　　2. C

翻譯練習題

1. 在那樣遙遠的國度生活，真是難以想像。
2. 那個行銷專家把最受歡迎的產品放在與眼睛同高之處，這樣你勢必會看到他們。

解答：

1. It's hard to imagine living in a faraway country like that.
2. The marketing specialist places the most popular products at eye level so that you cannot avoid seeing them.

關鍵句型 27：V1 ＋ to V2

V1		中文意思
bear/endure		忍受…
begin/start		開始…
cease		停止，不再…
continue		繼續…
dread		害怕…
expect		期待去…
hate		討厭…
hope	＋ to V2	希望去…
intend		打算…
learn		學習…
like/love		喜歡，喜愛…
plan		計劃要…
prefer		比較喜歡去…
stop		停下來去做…
want		想要去…
wish		想要去，希望去…

例 I <u>dread to think</u> what will happen if a thief breaks into our house.
如果小偷闖入我們家，我真不敢想會發生什麼事。

例 I <u>hate to say</u> goodbye and leave.
我討厭說再見道別。

例 After the criminal was caught, this incident had <u>ceased to be</u> news.
罪犯被逮捕後，這件事已不再是新聞了。

例 Will the female star <u>continue to work</u> after she gets married?
那個女明星結婚後會繼續工作嗎？

例 If I retire from my company, I <u>intend to</u> <u>open</u> a store as soon as I can.
如果我從公司退休,我打算盡快開家店。

例 To tell the truth, I <u>prefer to live</u> in a city. I don't like living in a quiet place.
老實說,我寧願生活在都市。我不喜歡住在安靜的地方。

例 Ingrid couldn't <u>bear to leave</u> her child and cried all the way to the airport.
英格麗忍受不了與孩子的離別之苦,去機場的路上一直在哭。

【注意】表示未來的名詞,其後也接不定詞 **(to + V)**。

例 After graduation, her <u>goal/dream/plan</u> is <u>to find</u> a good job.
畢業後她的目標/夢想/計畫是找到一份好工作。

例 The main <u>objective</u> of this advertisement is <u>to promote</u> the new product of our company.
這個廣告主要的目的是要推銷我們公司的新產品。

【注意】句 **only to** + **V**
　　　 = 句, **but** 句
　　　 結果卻是

例 He worked hard <u>only to be</u> fired.
　 = He worked hard, <u>but</u> he was fired.
　 他努力工作，結果卻被解雇。

文法練習題

1. I expect ＿＿＿＿ a call from you this week.
   (A) receive
   (B) received
   (C) receiving
   (D) to receive

2. I arrived at the train station in time
   ＿＿＿＿ I'd left my train ticket at home.
   (A) to find
   (B) found
   (C) only to find
   (D) but find

解答：　　**1. D**　　**2. C**

翻譯練習題

1. 這篇文章的作者想要引起對這個城市女性處境的關注。【使用 intend】
2. 他的偉大夢想就是成為一名職業搖滾音樂家。

解答：

1. The author of the article intended to draw attention to the situation faced by women in this city.
2. His big dream is to be a professional rock musician.

六、認識常見介系詞片語的用法

關鍵句型 1：介係詞by

【重點一】 by + V-ing 　藉由（表示透過…方法或手段）

= through (prep.利用；透過) + N

= by means of + N

例 By sending text messages, I can save a lot of money.

= Through text messages, I can save a lot of money.

= By means of text messages, I can save a lot of money.
藉由簡訊，我可以省很多錢。

【重點二】by 用在被動式裡，表「被…」

例 The book was translated by a famous linguist.
這本書是由知名語言學家所翻譯的。

例 I was almost hit by a ball while I was taking a walk in the park.
當我在公園散步時，我差點被一顆球打到。

【重點三】by + 交通工具

by + 交通工具	中文意思
by car	搭車,開車
by bus	搭公車
by train	搭火車
by subway/metro/tube	搭地鐵
by MRT	搭捷運
by plane/by air	搭飛機
by boat	搭船
by bicycle	騎單車
★例外的是:on foot (走路)	

例 (問) How do you go to work? 你怎麼上班?

(答) I go to work by MRT. 我搭捷運上班。

例 We traveled across Taiwan by bicycle last year.

我們去年騎單車環遊台灣。

【重點四】by + 時間　到了…;在…之前

例 The manager had to get there by Friday.
經理必須在周五前抵達那裡。

例 By the end of the day I had read over 2000 pages.
一天下來,我已經讀了超過兩千頁了。

【重點五】by 在…旁邊

例 When I am in trouble, he always stands by me.

當我有麻煩時,他總是守候在我身邊。

例 Please come here and sit by me.

請到這兒來坐在我旁邊。

文法練習題

1. I was attracted not _____ her beauty but _____ her good heart.
   - (A) with
   - (B) by
   - (C) in
   - (D) at

2. The salesman tries to earn his customers' trust _____ sending emails frequently.
   - (A) with
   - (B) to
   - (C) from
   - (D) by

解答: **1. B** **2. D**

翻譯練習題

1. 當記者到達旅館時,那個巨星已經搭乘大型華豪轎車去機場了。
2. 我比較喜歡靠窗的座位,因為我喜歡看雲飄過去。

解答：

1. By the time the reporters arrived at the hotel, the superstar had already gone to the airport by limousine.

2. I prefer a seat by the window because I like to watch the clouds pass by.

關鍵句型 2：介係詞 with

【重點一】表「跟…」

例 I hope to go to the party with you.
我希望跟你一起去派對。

例 I share the room with my friend so that I won't feel lonely.
我跟朋友共用一間房間，如此我不會覺得孤單。

【重點二】表「有了、帶著…」

例 With money, you can buy anything you like in the store.
有了錢你可以買這家店裡任何你喜歡的東西。

例 The man with white hair is my co-worker.
那個白頭髮的男人是我的同事。

【重點三】表「用…」

例 Lisa comes from America. She can't eat with chopsticks.
麗莎來自美國。她不會用筷子吃飯。

例 Your face is dirty. Please wipe it <u>with</u> a tissue.
你的臉很髒。請用面紙擦一擦。

【重點四】表「隨著…」

例 <u>With</u> the coming of summer, there are more and more people in the swimming pool.
隨著夏天的來到，游泳池裡的人越來越多。

例 The way she dresses will change <u>with</u> fashion.
她穿著打扮的方式會隨著時尚而改變。

【重點五】with + O + adj／分詞／介片　表附帶狀態

例 <u>With</u> swords drawn (pp) and ready (adj) to strike, the two swordsmen started colliding with each other several times.
拔出了劍，準備揮動，這兩個劍客開始多次的械鬥。

文法練習題

1. He was so angry that he hit me on the head ＿＿＿ his umbrella.
   (A) in
   (B) to
   (C) by
   (D) with

2. Mr. Wang walked slowly around the classroom, with his hands _____ behind his back.
   (A) fold
   (B) folds
   (C) folded
   (D) folding

3. _____ enough time I can get the hair done.
   (A) With
   (B) Without
   (C) If
   (D) Have

解答: 1. D   2. C   3. A

翻譯練習題

1. 每一次我去唱KTV時，我總是邀請我的好朋友跟我一起去。
2. 視力有可能隨著時間而變好嗎？
3. 隨著時間快速流逝，這裡的春天就快要來到了。

解答:

1. Every time (when) I go to KTV, I always invite my good friends to go with me.
2. Is it possible for vision to improve with time?
3. With time passing quickly, spring will be here soon.

關鍵句型 3：介係詞 as

【重點一】表「表身分」

例 Yo-Yo Ma is famous <u>as</u> an international cellist.
馬友友以國際大提琴家的身分而聞名。

例 <u>As</u> a doctor, your main duty is to cure people of their illnesses.
身為醫生你的主要職責就是替人治好疾病。

【重點二】與動詞「**work/serve/act/function**」合用

例 Miss Lin <u>works as</u> an English editor in that company.
林小姐在該公司裡擔任英文編輯。

例 This book can <u>serve as</u> a useful introduction to the research subject.
這本書可作為此研究主題的一個有用的入門。

【重點三】與動詞「**see/regard/think of/refer to/take**」合用

★**see/regard/think of/refer to/take + A + as + B**

把 A 視作為 B

例 I <u>regard</u> playing the guitar <u>as</u> a form of recreation.
我把彈吉他當作一種消遣。

例 She likes to be <u>referred to as</u> "Dr. Chen."
她喜歡以陳博士的身分自居。

文法練習題

1. In addition to her job at the publishing house, she works part-time ＿＿＿ a tutor.
   (A) to
   (B) as
   (C) at
   (D) of

2. Are the holes large enough to serve ＿＿＿ nests?
   (A) with
   (B) to
   (C) for
   (D) as

解答： 1. B 2. D

翻譯練習題

1. 阿妹受邀以特別來賓的身分出席演唱會。
2. 這個老先生總是穿著古怪，被鄰居視為怪人。

解答：

1. A-mei was invited to appear as special guest at the concert.
2. The old man always wears strange clothes and is regarded as eccentric by his neighbors.

關鍵句型 4：介係詞 for

【重點一】表「對…而言」

例 For me, it is very important to find a good job.
　對我來説，找一份好工作是非常重要的。

例 It is impossible for her to finish school by June this year.
　對她來説，今年六月之前完成學業是不可能的。

【重點二】表「替…，為了…人」

例 I am busy all day. I cook for my child, wash their clothes and also teach them to do their homework.
　我整天都很忙。我替我的小孩煮飯，洗衣服，還教他們做家課。

例 My parents are confident of my ability to find a job for myself.
　我的父母有自信我有能力替自己找到工作。

【重點三】表「因為…」

例 My friends used to laugh at me <u>for</u> being too timid.
我朋友以前常笑我過於膽小。

例 He often arrives late <u>for</u> a variety of reasons, so I don't believe him.
他常常由於種種原因遲到，所以我不相信他。

【重點四】**for** + 時間名詞，表「經歷…的時間」

例 After work, we often sit around the table, and talk <u>for</u> hours.
下班後，我們常圍坐在桌子旁邊，一聊就是數小時。

例 At work, the writer has to use his computer <u>for</u> a long time.
工作時，這位作家必須長時間使用他的電腦。

文法練習題

1. _____ fear of failing the final exam, I have no choice but to burn the midnight oil.
   (A) For
   (B) To
   (D) Despite
   (D) Out

2. It is necessary _____ me to have enough sleep.

Poor sleep may result in bad health.

(A) of

(B) in

(D) with

(D) for

解答： **1. A** **2. D**

翻譯練習題

1. 我們要怎樣才能報答父母親為我們所做的?
2. 自從結婚後,她已經很久不工作了。

解答：

1. How can we pay our parents back for what they have done to us?
2. Since she got married, she has been off work for a long time.

關鍵句型 5：介係詞 to

【重點一】表「對⋯而言」,與名詞「good/ harm」,以及形容詞「helpful grateful/thankful」合用

例 Eating more fruits will do good to you.
多吃水果對你有益。

例 Smoking has done considerable harm to your health.
抽菸已經對你的健康造成了很大的傷害。

例 Reading books has always been helpful to me.
看書一直對我很有幫助。

例 I was grateful to my mother for all that she had done.
我感激母親所做的一切。

【重點二】表「到…方面或領域」，與動詞「devote/dedicate，contribute，lead，relate，add，expose」合用

例 Miss Huang has devoted her whole life to benefiting the disadvantaged groups.
黃老師把一生都獻給了造福弱勢團體的事業。

例 Dr Ho's suggestion has greatly contributed to the accomplishment of our project.
何博士的建議對於我們企劃的完成功不可沒。

例 Drinking too much can lead to health problems.
飲酒過度會導致健康問題。

例 The psychologist asked me to relate what happened in my childhood to my present state of mind.

心理醫師要我把童年時的遭遇與目前的心境相聯起來。

例 This cup of coffee is bitter. Could you add some sugar to it?
這杯咖啡好苦。請你加些糖好嗎？

例 If I take off my coat and expose my bare arms to the terrible cold, I may start to cough.
如果我脫掉外套，在酷寒中露出雙臂，我可能會開始咳嗽。

【重點三】表「到…方面或領域」，與名詞
「key，answer，road，path，contribution，obstacle」合用

例 The police believe the missing wallet is the key to the murder.
警方認為那個遺失的錢包是偵破這宗謀殺案的線索。

例 What's the correct answer to Question Six?
第六題的正確答案是什麼？

例 This deal set me on the road to my first million.
這筆交易使我賺到頭一筆一百萬元。

例 His parents see a good job as his path to independence.
他的父母把一份好工作看作是他走向獨立的一條途徑。

例 Her parents' opposition is an obstacle to her dream of becoming a singer.

她父母的反對是她夢想成為歌手的障礙。

【重點四】表「到…地方,到…人」,與動詞「go/come/get/rush/return,send/deliver,happen」合用

例 After the gunshot injury, the two policemen were rushed to the hospital.

受到槍傷之後,這兩位受傷的警察被急忙送到醫院。

例 A mailman in a green uniform delivered the package to you this morning.

今天早上有一位穿綠色制服的郵差送這個包裹給你。

例 The book is due today. Remember to return it to the library after work.

這本書今天到期,下班後記得歸還給圖書館。

例 As soon as I get to Taichung, I'll call you.

我一到台中就會打電話給你。

例 He didn't want to tell me what had happened to him.

他不願意告訴我發生了什麼事。

【重點五】表「到…數目」，與動詞「**limit/re-strict，come/amount**」合用

例 If you don't feel like writing much, you can limit your essay answer to just 250 words instead of 400.

如果你不想寫太多，你可以把申論題答案限制在二百五十字以內，而非四百字。

例 Money lost through illness amounted to ten millions dollars.

因疾病而損失的金錢總計達到一千萬元。

【重點六】表「隨著旋律、音樂…」

★**dance to + the melody/tune/beat/music**
隨著旋律/曲子/節奏/音樂起舞

例 Come on! Let's dance to the beat.
來吧！讓我們隨著節奏起舞。

文法練習題

1. To prove my point, I told a story about what might happen _____ a person who becomes too lazy.

   (A) for

   (B) with

   (C) by

   (D) to

抓住文法句型翻譯寫作 就通了

2. This article was intended to draw attention
   to the fact that hard work is the only road
   _____ success.
   (A) for
   (B) with
   (C) by
   (D) to

解答： 1. D　　2. D

翻譯練習題

1. 成功是發揮自己的天賦及能力並且造福
   人群。
2. 她限制自己每天只喝一杯咖啡。

解答：

1. Success is applying your talents and
   abilities and make the most effective
   contribution to your fellow men.
2. She is restricting herself to a cup of coffee
   a day.

關鍵句型 6：介係詞 about

【重點一】表「關於…」

例 He has spent the last two years working on
   a project about new model of laptops.
   最近兩年他的時間都花在一個有關新型筆
   記型電腦的企劃案上。

例 There are rules in our class about changing seats.

在我們班換座位是有規定的。

【重點二】用在下列片語中

talk about	講到…
talk to 人 + about 事	找某人談談某事
give advice to 人 + on/about 事	給某人關於某事的建議
get into an argument with 人 + over/about 事	與某人爭論某事
think about	想到；考慮…
know about	知道…
worry about	擔心
hear about	聽說；得知…
bring about	導致，造成…
be serious about	對…認真看待
be curious about	對…好奇
be sure/certain + of/about	對…確定
be unsure/uncertain + of/about	對…不確定

例 The lecturer knew a lot about the subject; therefore, her speech was interesting.

關於這個主題演講者所知甚多，所以她的演講很有趣。

例 Although he was fired, he preferred not to think about the future at the moment.

雖然他被解雇，此時此刻他寧願不去想未來的事情。

例 Don't worry about the final exam. Just take it easy.
別擔心期末考了，就放輕鬆一點。

例 I am curious about the new film released last week.
我對上周上映的新電影感到好奇。

例 She got into an argument with her neighbors about the trash around her house.
她和她的鄰居因為在她家周遭的垃圾而吵了起來。

例 I want to talk to your parents about your performance at school.
我想和你的父母聊一下你在校的表現。

例 For me, the road to success is not easy because my parents are never serious about my dream.
對我來說成功之路並不平坦，因為我的父母從未認真看待我的夢想。

例 If you are unsure about the exam, ask your teacher to explain it.
如果你對考試有疑問，請你的老師講解一下。

文法練習題

1. She is a sensitive person. She might worry _____ things that haven't happened.
   - (A) about
   - (B) of
   - (C) to
   - (D) with

2. It is a story _____ what happened to his family during the earthquake.
   - (A) by
   - (B) for
   - (C) to
   - (D) about

解答： 1. A 2. D

翻譯練習題

1. 這篇研究論文著墨在男女之間的平等地位。
2. 語言的奇妙之處就在它具有深遠的影響力。

解答：

1. This research paper writes about the equal status between men and women.
2. The wonderful thing about language is its ability to have a profound influence.

關鍵句型 7：介係詞 on

【重點一】表「持續，進展」，與動詞「keep/go/move/work 合用

例 The mayor hasn't moved on any of the recommendations in the report.
市長尚未處理報告中的任何建議。

例 I haven't quite figured out the math problem yet, but I'm working on it.
我還沒有完全解決那道數學題，但我仍在努力中。

【重點二】表「關於…」

例 She published a book on job-hunting last month, and her best friend made some comments on it.
上個月她出版了一本有關求職的書，而她最好的朋友對它做出了一些評論。

例 In this post, I give some advice on how to become an effective leader.
這份工作我的職責是對於如何成為有效的領導者這方面給予一些建議。

【重點三】用在電器用品上

★ turn/switch + on 打開（電源、電器）
★ on + 電器產品（the phone/the computer/the Internet/the e-mail/the PDA）

例 I like to read on the PDA; it is like having a personal tutor.

我喜歡用個人數位助理器閱讀,就像是擁有私人家教老師。

例 We were watching TV when you called on the phone yesterday.

你昨天打電話來的時候,我們正在看電視。

例 If you use web mailbox, then the emails that you don't delete are stored on the email server.

如果你使用網路信箱,那麼那些你沒有刪除的信會被儲存在電子信件伺服器上。

【重點四】on + 日/節日/特定上下午晚

on + 日/節日/特定上下午晚	中文意思
on Sunday on Monday	在星期日 在星期一
on New Year's Day on Mother's Day	在元旦 在母親節
on holidays	在假日期間
on the first of February on the fifth of May	在二月一日 在五月五日
on the morning of June 22 on the evening of April 21	在六月二十二日的早晨 在四月二十一日的傍晚

例 In Taiwan, it is a custom to hold dragon boat races on Dragon Boat Festival.
台灣在端午節那天舉行划龍舟比賽是一種習俗。

例 Ferries going to the Cijin District of Kaohsiung City are packed with passengers on holidays.
每逢假日，往高雄旗津的渡輪擠滿了乘客。

文法練習題

1. Should I go ＿＿＿ doing the other exercise after I have finished this one?
   (A) of
   (B) on
   (C) to
   (D) about

2. I think it uncomfortable to type ＿＿＿ the iPad for extended periods.
   (A) in
   (B) to
   (C) on
   (D) of

解答： 1. B 2. C

翻譯練習題

1. 陳醫生對於身心健康的關聯性研究有興趣。
2. 很多家庭在母親節時團聚吃晚餐慶祝。

解答：

1. Dr. Chen is interested in the research topic on the link between mental and physical health.
2. Many families get together on Mother's Day to celebrate with dinner.

關鍵句型 8：介係詞 in

【重點一】 in ＋ 大地方

例 You must come see me in America some day.
有一天你一定要來美國看我。

例 Our school in Taipei is specifically designed to help learners study English.
我們在台北的學校是特別針對協助學習英文而設立的。

【重點二】 in ＋ 語言類單字

例 The beauty of her paintings cannot be described in words.
語言難以描述她的繪畫之美。

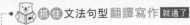

例 The document, written in Japanese, needs to be translated into Chinese first.

這份用日文寫成的文件需要先翻譯成中文。

【重點三】in + 上午、下午、傍晚/月份/季節/年代

in + 上午、下午、傍晚/月份/季節/年代	中文意思
in the morning in the afternoon in the evening	在早上 在下午 在晚上
in September	在九月
in spring in summer in fall／in autumn in winter	在春天 在夏天 在秋天 在冬天
in 2015 in the 1980s	在2015年 在一九八〇年代

【重點四】in + way (方法) 以…方法，以…方式

★ in + a + adj + way

例 The plot of the novel changed in an unexpected way.

這本小說的情節意外地轉變。

★ (in) this way （前面in可省略）如此一來 (= by doing so)

例 To marry a man, you must have more contact with him. <u>(In) this way</u>, you won't go very far wrong.

要嫁給一個男人，你必須多跟他接觸；這樣你就不會犯大錯了。

【重點五】**in** + 某方面

例 He is rich becaue he is very lucky <u>in</u> making money.

他很富有因為他在賺錢方面很幸運。

【重點六】**in** + **V-ing**，表「在做某事時」

例 Pedestrians must realise that <u>in crossing</u> the road against the red lights, they put their own safety in peril.

行人必須了解紅燈時穿越馬路對自身安全構成很大的危險。

【重點七】**in** + 衣服

例 She looked very beautiful <u>in that dress</u>.

她穿那件洋裝看起來很漂亮。

【重點八】與下列動詞(片語)合用：

tutor + 人 + in + 學科	輔導某人某學科
lose/bury/absorb + oneself + in + N/V-ing be + lost/buried/absorbed + in + N/V-ing	全神貫注於…，埋首於…
bathe in + N	沈浸在…
spare no effort in + N/V-ing	努力去…，盡力…
play a part/role + in + N/V-ing	在…扮演…的角色
make progress in + N/Ving	在…上有進步
do well in + 考試	…考試考得好
take pride in	在…方面感到自豪
differ in	在…方面不一樣
succeed in	在…方面成功
end up in	下場是…

例 My mother asked Miss Ho to tutor me in English.
媽媽請何老師教我英語。

例 He has absorbed himself in the book for two hours.
他已經全神貫注地讀這本書二小時了。

例 She likes playing the guitar. Music plays an important role in her daily lives.
她喜歡彈吉他。音樂在她日常生活中扮演重要的角色。

例 To succeed in passing the important exam, you have to continue to make progress in fighting against laziness.

為了順利通過這個重要的考試，你必須在對抗懶惰上持續精進。

例 Her classmates envies her because she does well in exams.

她的同學忌妒她，因為她考試成績好。

例 Her two children differs from each other in some aspects, but she takes great pride in both of them.

她的兩個孩子彼此有些差異，但是她對他們兩個都感到驕傲。

文法練習題

1. Since he can't speak Chinese, I try to talk to him _____ English.
   - (A) with
   - (B) of
   - (C) on
   - (D) in

2. _____ raising money to help the unprivileged, Helen made contact with many organisations that supported her ideas.
   - (A) To
   - (B) With

(C) In

(D) By

解答： 1. D 2. C

翻譯練習題

1. 一九五〇年代時流行的名字是什麼？
2. 婚禮上新郎穿著一套藍色禮服。

解答：

1. What are the popular names in the 1950s?
2. The bridegroom was dressed in a blue suit in the wedding ceremony.

關鍵句型 9：介係詞 at

【重點一】at ＋ 小地方

例 He was already waiting at the bus stop when I got there.
當我到達公車站時，他已在那等候。

例 I haven't seen you for a long time. Let's sit down at a corner table to chat.
我很久沒有看到你了。我們在角落的桌旁坐下來聊
天吧。

【重點二】at + 時刻／正午／半夜／年齡／聖誕節／日出／日落／上學，上班／用餐／處境／極限

at + 時間名詞	中文意思
at seven (o'clock)	七點
at seven-thirty	七點半
at 11:15	十一點十五分
at + the/that + point/ moment/time	在那時；當時
at noon	中午
at night	夜晚
at midnight	半夜
at Christmas	聖誕節
at sunrise	日出
at sunset	日落
at school	還在就學
at work	工作中
at breakfast	在吃早餐
at lunch	在吃中餐
at dinner	在吃晚餐
at war at risk at peace at large	在戰爭中 處於危險中 已過世 自由的、逍遙的、 未被捕的
at least	至少
at worst	最壞的情況

例 I graduated from high school last year. At that time, I was still living at home.
我去年從中學畢業。當時,我仍住在家裡。

例 I used to get up at six and play basketball for half an hour every day.
我以前曾經每天早上六點起床打籃球半小時。

例 The earthquake happened at midnight and caused a lot of damage.
地震於半夜發生,造成很大的損傷。

例 Some of the most beautiful views in the mountains are seen at either sunrise or sunset.
在山裡一些最美的景色不是在日出就是在日落時出現。

【注意】時間表示比較表

in the morning	= 1:00 A.M. to noon	凌晨一點到中午
in the afternoon	= noon to about 5:00 P.M.	中午到大約下午五點
in the evening	= about 5:00 P.M. to 9:00 P.M.	大約下午五點到晚上九點
at night	= about 7:00 P.M. to after midnight	大約晚上七點到半夜後
★ at noon = at 12:00 P.M.		
★ at midnight = at 12:00 A.M.		

【重點三】用在下列的片語裡，表「對著…，對於…」

look at	看著…
shout at	對著…叫喊
laugh at	嘲笑
aim at	瞄準，目的是…
excel + in/at	擅長於…
be good at be bad at	擅長於… 不擅長…
be shocked at	對…感到震驚
wonder + at/about	對…感到驚訝
be disappointed + at/with/about	對…感到失望

例 This anti-drug campaign is mainly aimed at college students.
這場反毒運動主要是針對大學生。

例 I am deeply disappointed at the approach taken by our company in dealing with this issue.
對於我們公司在處理這件爭議上採取的方法，我感到深深失望。

例 Parents are shocked at the widespread availability of wine in our dormitory.
爸媽對於我們宿舍裡酒那麼容易取得感到震驚。

文法練習題

1. He is good _____ math, while I fail in most math quizzes and monthly exams.
   (A) in
   (B) at
   (C) to
   (D) for

2. The bus will pick up and drop off passengers _____ any bus stop along the route.
   (A) on
   (B) in
   (C) at
   (D) with

解答： 1. B 2. C

翻譯練習題

1. 飛機將在早上七點起飛。
2. 她的論文旨在發展字彙教學的一般性方法。[用 aim at]

解答：

1. The plane will take off at seven o'clock in the morning.
2. Her thesis aims at developing general methods for teaching vocabulary.

關鍵句型 10：與數字有關的介係詞

【重點一】at + 與數字有關的名詞 (speed/rate/price/cost/expense/age/eye level)

at + 與數字有關的名詞	中文意思
at + a/the + speed/rate + of	以…速度
at + the + expense + of at 人's expense at great/little/no expense	以…為代價 由某人付費 花費很多/花費微薄/不用花費
at a cost of at all costs (= whatever happens)	以…價格 不惜任何代價
at + the + age + of	…歲
at eye level	和眼睛同高的位置

例 Success in job market is often achieved at the expense of health.
職場上的成功常常是以健康為代價的。

例 Linda has just been on an English course, all at the company's expense.
琳達剛開始上一個英文課程,費用全部由公司支付。

例 To celebrate their wedding anniversary, they held the party at great expense.
為了慶祝結婚周年紀念日,他們花大錢辦了派對。

例 The repair of the kitchen is going up at a cost of ten thousand dollars.
這間廚房的維修要花費一萬元。

例 I drive to a town 30 miles away at an average speed of 50 miles per hour.
我以平均每小時五十英里的速度行駛到一個三十英里遠的城鎮。

例 He left home at the age of 18. That's why he's so independent.
他十八歲那年離開家。那就是為何他如此獨立。

【重點二】 about/around + 數字　大約…數字
(= 數字 + or so)
(= some + 數字)

例 It takes about two hours to reach the airport from my house.
從我家到機場大概要花兩小時。

例 At around 5:35 p.m. we have to do the sweeping and
cleaning in the classroom.

大約在下午五點三十五分時，我們必須在教室裡做打掃和清潔。

【重點三】over + 數字 (= more then + 數字)
超過⋯數字

例 This book has been translated into more than five languages and is sold in over ten countries.

這本書已經被翻譯成五個語言以上，並在超過十個以上的國家銷售。

【重點四】by表差額

例 I missed the train by 15 minutes.
我晚了十五分鐘沒趕上那班火車。

例 He argued with the waiter for ten minutes because he was overcharged by 10 dollars.
他跟服務生吵了十分鐘，因為他被多收了十塊錢。

文法練習題

1. It may help the sale of these CDs if you put them up ＿＿＿ eye level with a nice review for the customer to read.
   (A) by
   (B) at
   (C) in
   (D) for

2. It is estimated that <u>some</u> 50 passengers were left stranded at the port.
   (A) or
   (B) so
   (C) about
   (D) near

解答： 1. B　　2. C

翻譯練習題

1. 這個學校具有五十年以上的歷史，以商業教育而聞名。
2. 這間公寓以新台幣五百萬元賣出。

解答：

1. This school has a history of over fifty years and is well-known for commercial education.
2. This apartment was sold at a price of NTD five million dollars.

關鍵句型 11：介係詞 besides, except

介係詞（片語）	中文意思
besides (= in addition to) (= apart from) (= aside from)	除了…之外還有（將後方的人/事/物「包含在內」）
except (= apart from) (= aside from)	除了…之外，其他都…（將後方的人/事/物「排除在外」）
except for (= apart from) (= aside from)	除了…之外，其他都…（將後方的人/事/物「排除在外」）

【注意一】except 和 except for 大致上可通用，兩者之間細微的差別在於except 常用來談論相同的東西，而 except for 則用於談論不同的東西，並隱含惋惜之意。再者，except通常不放句首，而except for則可放句首。

【注意二】besides 也可當副詞轉折詞，表「此外」：(= in addition = moreover = furthermore = what's more)

例 My cat is mild and tame. Besides, it can catch mice.
我的貓溫和又順從。此外它還會抓老鼠。

例 Mr. and Mrs. Lin raise ten dogs. <u>In addition to</u> their own six dogs, they have fostered four dogs.

林先生和林太太養了十隻狗。除了他們本身的六隻狗,他們已經領養了四隻狗。

例 He can have any of the pens <u>except</u> this one.

他可以拿任何一支筆,但這支除外。

例 <u>Except for</u> several grammatical mistakes, your English composition is good overall.

除了幾個文法錯誤外,你的英文作文整體而言很不賴。

解答:

1. <u>Besides</u> going to Japanese classes three times a week, she does yoga on Fridays.
   - (A) Despite
   - (B) In addition to
   - (C) Beside
   - (D) Except for

2. <u>Except for</u> one young student and me, this MRT carriage was empty.
   - (A) In spite of
   - (B) In addition to
   - (C) Aside from
   - (D) Without

解答： 1. B 2. C

翻譯練習題

1. 曼蒂是一個好女人，唯一可挑剔的是她的神經質。
   【用except for】

2. 除了圖書總館之外，這個城市還有任何分館嗎？
   【用in addition to】

解答：

1. Mandy is a good woman, except for her nervousness.

2. Are there any branch libraries in this city in addition to the General Library?

附錄：【基礎時態大補帖】

一、現在簡單式

【重點一】使用時機：

(一) 表示現在的動作或狀態

例 Mary sings very well.
瑪莉唱歌很好聽。

例 John likes to play basketball.
約翰喜歡打籃球。

例 It rains a lot in Taipei.
台北多雨。

例 She is an English teacher.
她是一個英文老師。

(二) 不變的事實或真理

例 The sun rises in the east.
太陽從東邊上升。

例 The earth goes around the sun.
地球繞著太陽跑。

例 Water freezes at zero degrees Centigrade.
水攝氏零度時結冰。

例 Knowledge is power.
知識就是力量。

(三) 表示一種習慣 (常與頻率副詞或時間副詞連用)

★ 頻率副詞：**always** (總是)，**often** (常常)，**usually**

(經常)，**sometimes** (有時候)，**seldom** (很少)，**never** (從不)

★ 時間副詞: **every + morning/summer/ Sunday/day**

(每個早上/每個夏天/每個星期天/每天)

例 I often go to the movies every Sunday (= on Sundays).
我常在周日去看電影。

例 My father goes jogging every morning.
我爸爸每天早上慢跑。

例 I usually go to work by bus.
我經常搭公車上班。

例 She always plays the guitar when she is free.
她有空時就彈吉他。

例 He never takes a rest after lunch.
他午餐後從不休息。

例 David takes a trip every summer.
大衛夏天都會去旅行。

例 Mark seldom plays baseball with his son.
馬克很少跟他的兒子打棒球。

例 They are often late for class.
他們上課常常遲到。

【重點二】現在簡單式裡動詞的變化：

1. 主詞 (you/we/they/複數主詞) + 原形動詞

例 They take exercise every evening.
他們傍晚都會去運動。

例 My classmates play baseball every day.
我的同學每天打棒球。

例 We sometimes listen to the music when we are free.
我們有空的時候有時候會聽音樂。

2. 主詞 (he/she/it/單數主詞)
+ 動詞 (字尾加上 s 或 es，或去 y 加上 ies)

【注意】不規則變化「have→has」

例 Vicky drinks tea every day.
維琪每天喝茶。

　　【原形動詞 drink，字尾加上 s】

例 He goes to work by MRT every morning.
他每天早上搭捷運去上班。

　　【原形動詞 go，字尾加上 es】

例 She studies English every Saturday.
她每週六學習英文。

【原形動詞study，去掉字尾y加上ies】

3. 變化表：

一般動詞 （原形）	現在簡單式 （字尾加s）	中文意思	變化後 動詞的音標
close	closes	關上	[klosɪz]
move	moves	移動， 搬家	[muvz]
like	likes	喜歡	[laɪks]
use	uses	使用	[jusɪz]
open	opens	打開	[ˋopənz]
play	plays	玩	[plez]
talk	talks	說話	[tɔks]
ask	asks	問	[æsks]
jump	jumps	跳	[dʒʌmps]
call	calls	打電話， 稱呼	[kɔlz]
listen	listens	聽	[ˋlɪsənz]
do	does	做	[dʌz]
go	goes	去	[goz]
pass	passes	經過	[pæsɪz]
buzz	buzzes	嗡嗡叫	[bʌzɪz]
watch	watches	觀看	[watʃɪz]
wash	washes	洗	[waʃɪz]

一般動詞 (原形)	現在簡單式 (去y加上ies) 【註解：動詞字尾是「子音＋y」時，須先去掉y，再加 ies】	中文 意思	變化後 動詞的音標
fly	flies	飛	[flaɪz]
study	studies	學習，研究	[ˋstʌdɪz]
try	tries	嘗試	[traɪz]

【注意】主詞 + be動詞 (am／is／are) + N／adj／介片〔也為現在簡單式〕

例 I am very fond of music.
我很喜歡音樂。

【重點三】現在簡單式的疑問句型：

1. Do + 主詞 (you/I/we/they/複數名詞) + 原形動詞...?

例 Do you play basketball after school every day?
你每天放學後打籃球嗎？

例 Do they go jogging every morning?
他們每天早上去慢跑嗎？

例 Do John and Mary go to work by MRT?
約翰和瑪莉搭捷運上班嗎？

2. **Does** + 主詞 (he/she/it/單數名詞) + 原形動詞…?

例 Does Lisa play the piano?
麗莎彈鋼琴嗎？

例 Does he go to the concert every month?
他每個月去音樂會嗎？

例 Does it rain a lot in Taiwan?
台灣多雨嗎？

3. **Be**動詞 (Am／Is／Are) + 主詞 + N／adj／介片?

例 Is the picture on the wall beautiful?
牆上的照片美嗎？

【重點四】現在簡單式的否定句型：

1. 主詞 (you/I/we/they/複數名詞) + **do not**／**don't** + 原形動詞...

例 I don't cook dinner every evening.
我沒有每個晚上煮飯。

例 They don't have a car.
他們沒有車。

2. 主詞 (he/she/it/單數名詞) + **does not**／**doesn't** + 原形動詞...

例 Helen doesn't like to sing songs in English.
海倫不喜歡用英文唱歌。

例 He <u>doesn't</u> drive to work.
他不開車上班。

3. 主詞 + be動詞 (am／is／are) + not +
   N／adj／介片

例 We <u>are not</u> basketball players.
我們不是籃球員。

範例短文 「現在簡單式」

Losing Weight

It seems that my husband has to lose weight. I find him not at ease when he joins in public activities. He looks diffident when he talks to new friends. Besides, it takes him a lot of efforts to put on a T-shirt and pants because he is just too fat. I remember helping him buckle the buttons many times. And sometimes I see him slip and fall, but can't quickly pick himself up. Our best friend Annie keeps persuading my husband to see a doctor. She also suggests that he eat more vegetables and exercise more. I consider it necessary for him to stop eating fried and sweet junk foods, too. Butit takes us lots of patience and love to communicate with him. Usually he prefers to sleep and eat rather than exercise. He is used to being fat. Yet we will continue to use many terrible examples to persuade him and spend more time making him aware of the harm of losing health and confidence if he keeps a heavy weight.

減肥

　　我的老公似乎必須減肥。我發現他參加公開活動時不自在。當他跟新朋友說話時也顯得沒有自信。此外，他穿T恤或是長褲時好費勁，因為他實在太胖了。我記得幫他扣上鈕扣好多次。有時候我看見他滑倒，卻無法很快自己爬起來。

　　我最好的朋友安妮一直勸我先生要去看醫生。她也建議他多吃蔬菜和多運動。我認為他有必要停止食用油炸及甜的垃圾食物。但跟他溝通花費我們好多耐心和愛心。通常他偏愛睡覺跟吃東西，而非運動。他已經習慣肥胖了。然而我們會繼續使用很多恐怖的例子來說服他，也會花更多時間讓他知道失去健康跟自信的危害，如果他持續肥胖的話。

範例短文 「現在簡單式」

Music Lovers

My name is Kelly. I like music a lot. I often play the piano on weekends, and I practice the guitar every day. My roommate May likes music, too. She is an elementary school teacher, and she teaches music at a school. She always plays the piano when she has free time. However, she doesn't like to sing because she thinks her voice is not good. But she listens to pop songs and classical music every night after work. Sometimes we practice the piano together, but we don't sing songs together. All of our friends call us "music lovers," because we both love music so much.

音樂愛好者

　　我的名字是凱莉。我很喜歡音樂。我常常在週末彈鋼琴，而且我每天練習吉他。我的室友梅也喜歡音樂。她是一個國小老師，她在學校教音樂。她有空時總是彈鋼琴。然而，她不喜歡唱歌，因為她覺得自己的歌喉不好。但是她每天晚上下班後聽流行音樂跟古典音樂。有時候我們一起練習鋼琴，但是沒有一起唱歌。所有我們的朋友都說我們是「音樂愛好者」，因為我們兩個都這麼喜愛音樂。

【練習題】

I. 中翻英
1. 你喜歡喝茶嗎?
2. 英格麗喜歡彈鋼琴。
3. 我爸媽每天早上去公園散步。
4. 他們每年出國一次嗎?
5. 她每周二晚上上吉他課。

II. 請找出（範例短文：Losing Weight）一文中有運用到「現在簡單式句型」的句子，並將該部分劃上底線。

III. 請找出（範例短文：Music Lovers）一文中有運用到「現在簡單式否定句型」的句子，並將該部分劃上底線。

IV. 選擇題

1. Water _____ at 100 degrees Centigrade.
   - (A) boiled
   - (B) is boiled
   - (C) boils
   - (D) boiling

2. I _____ to the concert every two months.
   - (A) went
   - (B) going
   - (C) go
   - (D) am going

3. _____ your students like English?
   - (A) Do
   - (B) Does
   - (C) Are
   - (D) Is

4. Sally _____ the dishes after dinner.
   - (A) don't wash
   - (B) doesn't wash
   - (C) wash
   - (D) be washing

5. Mr. Ho _____ two cars now.
   - (A) have
   - (B) has
   - (C) had
   - (D) is having

解答：

I.

1. Do you like to drink tea?
2. Ingrid likes to play the piano.
3. My parents take a walk in the park every morning.
4. Do they go abroad once a year?
5. She goes to the guitar class every Tuesday (= on Tuesdays).

II.

1. It seems that my husband has to lose weight.
   〔*have／has + to + V 表「必須」，也為現在簡單式〕

2. I find him not at ease when he joins in public activities.

3. He looks diffident when he talks to new friends.

4. Besides, it takes him a lot of efforts to put on a T-shirt and pants because he is just too fat.

5. I remember helping him buckle the buttons many times.

6. And somctimes I see him slip and fall, but can't quickly pick himself up.〔*can／can't + V 表「可以／不能…」，也為現在簡單式〕

7. Our best friend Annie keeps persuading my husband to see a doctor.

8. She also suggests that he eat more vegetables and exercise more.〔*eat 和 exercise前面省略了should，這裡的that句也為現在簡單式。〕

9. I consider it necessary for him to stop eating fried and sweet junk foods, too.

10. But it takes us lots of patience and love to communicate with him.

11. Usually he prefers to sleep and eat rather than exercise.

12. He is used to being fat.

13. Yet we will continue to use many terrible examples to persuade him and spend more time making him aware of the harm of losing health and confidence if he keeps a heavy weight.

III.

1. However, she doesn't like to sing because she thinks her voice is not good.

2. Sometimes we practice the piano together, but we don't sing songs together.

IV. CCABB

二、過去簡單式

【重點一】be動詞的過去式

(一) be 動詞「現在式」與「過去式」對應表

be動詞現	音標	be動詞過	音標
am	[æm]	**was**	[wɑz]
is	[ɪz]	**was**	[wɑz]
are	[ɑr]	**were**	[wɝ]

(二) 常與「過去時間副詞(片語)」連用，常見的有：

1. **yesterday** (昨天)，**before** (以前)，**just now** (剛才)

2. **yesterday morning/afternoon/evening** 昨天早上/下午/晚上

3. **the day before yesterday** 前天

4. **last night/week/month/year** 昨晚/上週/上個月/去年

5. 一段時間 + **ago**

例 She was sick yesterday.
她昨天生病。

例 David was a magician before.
大衛以前是魔術師。

例 My parents were home last night.
我父母昨晚在家。

例 We were busy last month.
上個月我們很忙。

例 My mother went shopping yesterday afternoon.
我媽媽昨天下午去購物。

【重點二】一般動詞的過去式

1. 規則變化：字尾加 **d**、**ed**、去 y 加 **ied**，或重複字尾再加上 **ed**，常見的如下表：

一般動詞 (原形)	過去式(字尾加d)	中文意思	過去式動詞 的音標
close	closed	關上	[klozd]
move	moved	移動，搬家	[muvd]
like	liked	喜歡	[laɪkt]
use	used	使用	[just]
一般動詞 (原形)	字尾加ed	中文意思	過去式動詞 的音標
open	opened	打開	[ˋopənd]
play	played	玩	[pled]
talk	talked	說話	[tɔkt]
ask	asked	問	[æskt]
jump	jumped	跳	[dʒʌmpt]
wash	washed	洗	[waʃt]
call	called	打電話， 稱呼	[kɔld]
listen	listened	聽	[ˋlɪsənd]
watch	watched	觀看	[watʃt]
一般動詞 (原形)	字尾加ied【註解：動詞字尾是「子音＋y」時，須先去掉 y，再加 ied】	中文意思	過去式動詞 的音標
fly	flied	飛	[flaɪd]
study	studied	學習，研究	[ˋstʌdɪd]
try	tried	嘗試	[traɪd]
一般動詞 (原形)	重複字尾再加上ed【註解：動詞字尾呈「子音 ＋ 母音 ＋ 子音」排列時，則須重覆字尾，再加 ed】	中文意思	過去式動詞 的音標
drop	dropped	滴下，掉下	[drapt]
jog	jogged	慢跑	[dʒagd]
stop	stopped	停止	[stapt]

2. 不規則變化：只能背熟，看到一個就記一個。常見的如下表：

原形動詞	音標	過去式	音標
buy（買）	[baɪ]	bought	[bɔt]
come（來）	[kʌm]	came	[kem]
do（做）	[du]	did	[dɪd]
go（去）	[go]	went	[wɛnt]
give（給）	[gɪv]	gave	[gev]
make（製造）	[mek]	made	[med]
read（閱讀；看書）	[rid]	read	[rɛd]
run（跑）	[rʌn]	ran	[ræn]
see（看；看見）	[si]	saw	[sɔ]
sit（坐）	[sɪt]	sat	[sæt]
speak（說）	[spik]	spoke	[spok]
teach（教；教書）	[titʃ]	taught	[tɔt]
wear（穿）	[wɛr]	wore	[wor]
hear（聽）	[hɪr]	heard	[hɝd]
catch（抓；捉）	[kætʃ]	caught	[kɔt]
drink（喝）	[drɪŋk]	drank	[dræŋk]
eat（吃）	[it]	ate	[et]
find（發現；找到）	[faɪnd]	found	[faʊnd]
get（獲得）	[gɛt]	got	[gɑt]
have（有；吃；喝）	[hæv]	had	[hæd]
put（放置）	[pʊt]	put	[pʊt]
ride（騎）	[raɪd]	rode	[rod]
say（說）	[se]	said	[sɛd]
sell（賣）	[sɛl]	sold	[sold]

原形動詞	音標	過去式	音標
sing（唱；唱歌）	[sɪŋ]	sang	[sæŋ]
sleep（睡覺）	[slip]	slept	[slɛpt]
stand（站立）	[stænd]	stood	[stʊd]
take（拿；搭乘）	[tek]	took	[tʊk]
write（寫）	[raɪt]	wrote	[rot]
forget（忘記）	[fɚ˙gɛt]	forgot	[fɚ˙gɑt]
grow（成長；種植）	[gro]	grew	[gru]
pay（付錢）	[pe]	paid	[ped]

【重點三】過去簡單式的否定句

(一) 過去式 be 動詞 + **not** = 否定句 =「不是」

★ was not 可縮寫成 wasn't [˙wɑzənt]

★ were not 可縮寫成 weren't [wɝnt]

(二) 主詞 + **didn't** + 原形動詞...

★ didn't [˙dɪdənt] = did not

【did 為助動詞 do 的過去式，在此的功用為協助一般動詞「造否定句」。】

例 It was not cold yesterday. It was hot.
昨天天氣不冷。昨天天氣炎熱。

例 They were not in Taipei last year. They were in Kaohsiung.
去年他們不在台北。他們在高雄。

例 I didn't play basketball last month.
上個月我沒有打籃球。

例 Lisa didn't clean her room last week.
麗莎上個禮拜沒有打掃房間。

【重點四】過去簡單式的疑問句

(一) 有過去式 be 動詞的句子

1. 將「主詞 + 過去式 be 動詞」 改為「過去式 be 動詞 + 主詞...?」

★要記得將句尾改成問號「？」

例 (肯定句) Lession Six was difficult.
第六課很難。

→ (疑問句) Was Lession Six difficult?
第六課很難嗎？

例 (肯定句) They were fat three years ago.
三年前他們很胖。

→(疑問句) Were they fat three years ago?
三年前他們很胖嗎？

2. 回答時，可用簡答或詳答的方式：

(1) 肯定簡答：Yes, 代名詞 + 過去式 be 動詞.
肯定詳答：Yes, (代名詞 + 過去式 be 動詞.) + 句子。

例 Was his wife a teacher before?
他老婆以前是老師嗎？

→ (肯定簡答) Yes, she was.
是的，她是。

→ (肯定詳答 1) Yes, she was a teacher
before.

是的,她以前是老師。

→ (肯定詳答 2) Yes, she was. She was
a teacher before.

是的,她是。她以前是老師。

例 Were they students two years ago?
(疑問句) 兩年前他們是學生嗎?

→ (肯定簡答) Yes, they were.
是的,他們是。

→ (肯定詳答 1) Yes, they were students two
years ago.

是的,他們兩年前是學生。

→ (肯定詳答 2) Yes, they were. They were
students two years ago.

是的,他們是。他們兩年前是學生。

(2) 否定簡答:No, 代名詞 + 過去式be動詞
+ not (可用 縮寫體)。

否定詳答:No, (代名詞 + 過去式be動詞
+ not (可用縮寫體).) + 否定句子。

例 Was his wife a teacher before?
他老婆以前是老師嗎?

→ (否定簡答) No, she was not. (或 No, she
wasn't.)

不,她不是。

→ (否定詳答 1) No, she was not
　(或 wasn't) a teacher before.
　不，她以前不是老師。

→ (否定詳答 2) No, she was not.
　(或 No, she wasn't.)
　She was not a teacher before.
　不，她不是。她以前不是老師。

例 Were they students two years ago?
　(疑問句) 兩年前他們是學生嗎？

→ (否定簡答) No, they were not.
　(或 No, they weren't.)
　不，他們不是。

→ (否定詳答 1) No, they were not
　(或 weren't) students two years ago .
　不，他們兩年前不是學生。

→ (否定詳答 2) No, they were not.
　(或 No, they weren't.) They were not
　students two years ago.
　不，他們不是。他們兩年前不是學生。

(二) 有一般動詞的句子

1. Did ＋ 主詞 ＋ 原形動詞...?

★ did為助動詞do的過去式，在此的功用為
　協助一般動　詞「造疑問句」。

例 (肯定句) Mary met him in the park last
　week.
　瑪莉上週在公園遇見他。

→ (疑問句) <u>Did Mary meet</u> him in the park
last week?

瑪莉上週在公園遇見他嗎?

例 (肯定句) She went to the concert yesterday.
她昨天去音樂會。

→ (疑問句) <u>Did she go</u> to the concert
yesterday?

她昨天有去音樂會嗎?

2. 回答時,可用簡答或詳答的方式:

(1) 肯定簡答:Yes, 代名詞 + did.
肯定詳答:Yes, (代名詞 + did.) + 句子.

例 Did Mary meet him in the park last week?
瑪莉上週在公園遇見他嗎?

→ (肯定簡答) Yes, she did.
是的,她是。

→ (肯定詳答 1) Yes, she met him in the park
last week.

是的,她上週在公園遇見他。

→ (肯定詳答 2) Yes, she did. She met him
in the park last week.

是的,她是。她上週在公園遇見他。

(2) 否定簡答:No, 代名詞 + did + not
(可用縮寫體).
否定詳答:No, (代名詞 + did + not
(可用縮寫體).)+ 否定句子。

例 Did you go to the concert yesterday?
你昨天有去音樂會嗎?

→ (否定簡答) No, I did not. (或 No, I didn't.)

不，我沒有。

→ (否定詳答 1) No, I didn't go to the concert yesterday.

不，我昨天沒有去音樂會。

→ (否定詳答 2) No, I did not. (或 No, I didn't.) I didn't go to the concert yesterday.

不，我沒有。我昨天沒有去音樂會。

範例短文 「過去簡單式」

My Birthday Last Year

My birthday last year is unforgettable. I was born on September 8th. My friends and family held a birthday party for me on that day last year in my house. They prepared a lot of foods and drinks. And they even invited my favorite teacher to the party. Moreover, some of my friends performed my favorite English songs, and I really enjoyed their performance. We all had a good time together. And I was very happy and cried tears of joy at the end of the party.

我去年的生日

　　我去年的生日令人難忘。我出生於九月八日。我朋友和家人去年在那一天在我家替我舉行了生日派對。他們準備了很多食物和飲料。他們甚至邀請我最喜歡的老師來。而且我的一些朋友還表演了我最喜歡的英文歌曲，我真的很喜愛他們的表演。我們一起度過了美好的時光。我非常開心，在派對結束時喜極而泣。

【練習題】

I. 連貫式翻譯 (一)

1. 我母親出生於一月17日。今年六十歲。
2. 她以前是個護士。
3. 去年三月她從一家醫院退休。
4. 我們在三月底時替她舉行了慶祝派對。
5. 那天她非常開心。

II. 連貫式翻譯 (二)

1. 大衛以前是個籃球員。
2. 放學後他常和同學一起練習籃球。
3. 三年前他從學校畢業。
4. 畢業後，他在電腦公司工作。
5. 因為工作太忙，去年一整年他都沒有打籃球。

III. 請找出（範例短文：**My Birthday Last Year**）一文中有運用到本單元教學討論的「過去式」的句型，並將該部分劃上底線。

解答

I.

1. My mother was born on January 17th. She is sixty years old now.
2. She was a nurse before.
3. She retired from a hospital last March.
4. We held a celebration party for her at the end of last March.
5. She was very happy on that day. (或 She had a good time on that day.)

II.

1. David was a basketball player before.
2. He often practiced basketball with his classmates
   after school.
3. He graduated from school three years ago.
4. After graduation, he worked in a computer company.
5. Because he was too busy with his work, he didn't play basketball the whole year last year.

III.

1. I <u>was</u> born on September 8th.
2. My friends and family <u>held</u> a birthday party for me on that day last year in my house.
3. They <u>prepared</u> a lot of foods and drinks.
4. And they even <u>invited</u> my favorite teacher to the party.
5. Moreover, some of my friends <u>performed</u> my favorite English songs, and I really <u>enjoyed</u> their performance.
6. We all <u>had</u> a good time together.
7. And I <u>was</u> very happy and <u>cried</u> tears of joy at the end of the party.

三、現在進行式

【重點一】現在進行式的句型需要用到現在分詞 **(V-ing)**。

1. 現在進行式: 主詞 + be動詞 + **V-ing**
   【某人正在⋯】

例 My children <u>are playing</u> in the park.
   我們小孩正在公園玩。

例 He <u>is eating</u> breakfast.
   他正在吃早餐。

例 My father <u>is singing</u> in the bathroom.
   我爸爸正在浴室唱歌。

例 I <u>am brushing</u> my teeth.
我正在刷牙。

2. 現在進行式的疑問句型：

(1) Be動詞 ＋ 主詞 ＋ V-ing...?【某人正在…?】

(肯定簡答) Yes, 主詞 ＋ be動詞.【是的，某人是。】

(肯定詳答) Yes, (主詞 ＋ be動詞.) 主詞 ＋ be動詞 ＋ V-ing...【是的，(某人是。) 某人正在…】

例 Is it raining?　正在下雨嗎？
(肯定簡答) Yes, it is.　是的。
(肯定詳答1) Yes, it is raining.　是的，正在下雨。
(肯定詳答2) Yes, it is. It is raining.
是的，沒錯。正在下雨。

例 Are they playing in the playground?
他們正在操場玩嗎？
(肯定簡答) Yes, they are. 是的，他們是。
(肯定詳答1) Yes, they are playing in the playground. 是的，他們正在操場玩。
(肯定詳答2) Yes, they are. They are playing in the playground.
是的，他們是，他們正在操場玩。

(2) Be動詞 + 主詞 + **V-ing...?** 【某人正在…？】

(否定簡答) No, 主詞 + be動詞 + not (可用縮寫體). 【不，某人不是。】

(否定詳答) No, (主詞 + be動詞 + not.) (可用縮寫體) 主詞 + be動詞 + not + V-ing...

【不，(某人不是。) 某人沒有正在…】

例 Is John taking a bath? 約翰正在洗澡嗎？

(否定簡答) No, he is not (或isn't). 不，他沒有。

(否定詳答 1) No, he is not taking a bath. 不，他沒有正在洗澡。

(否定詳答 2) No, he is not (或isn't). He is not taking a bath. 不，他沒有，他沒有正在洗澡。

例 Are your students reading English books? 你的學生正在讀英文書嗎？

(否定簡答) No, they are not (或aren't). 不，他們沒有。

(否定詳答 1) No, they are not reading English books.

不，他們沒有正在讀英文書。

（否定詳答 **2**）No, they are not（或aren't）. They are not reading English books.

不，他們沒有，他們沒有正在讀英文書。

【重點二】疑問詞開頭的現在進行式句型

1. **(問) What + be**動詞 + 主詞 + **V-ing...?**【某人正在…？】

   (答) 主詞 + **be**動詞 + **Ving...**【某人正在…】

例 (問) What are you doing?

   你正在做甚麼？

   (答) I am playing the guitar.

   我正在彈吉他。

例 (問) What is your mother doing?

   你的母親正在做甚麼？

   (答) She is cooking dinner.

   她正在煮晚餐。

例 (問) What is Kevin reading?

   凱文正在讀甚麼？

   (答) He is reading a magazine.

   他正在讀雜誌。

例 (問) What are the students studying?

   這些學生正在讀甚麼？

   (答) They are studying math.

   他們正在讀數學。

2. (問) Who + is + V-ing...?【誰正在…？】
(簡答) 主詞 + be動詞.【是某人】
(詳答) 主詞 + be動詞 + V-ing...【某人正在…】

例 (問) Who is singing?　誰在唱歌？
(簡答) Vicky is.　是維琪。

例 (詳答) Vicky is singing.　維琪正在唱歌
(問) Who is washing the clothes?　誰正在洗衣服？
(簡答) My students are.　是我的學生們。
(詳答) My students are washing the clothes.
我們學生們正在洗衣服。

例 (問) Who is talking on the phone?　誰正在講電話？
(簡答) Jane is.　是珍。
(詳答) Jane is talking on the phone.　珍正在講電話。

例 (問) Who is playing the piano?　誰正在彈鋼琴？
(簡答) My younger sister is.　是我妹妹。
(詳答) My younger sister is playing the piano.
我妹妹正在彈鋼琴。

【重點三】Look!或Listen!開頭

1. **Look!** + 現在進行式的句子
2. **Listen!** + 現在進行式的句子

例 Look! They <u>are playing</u> basketball.
瞧！他們正在打籃球。

例 Listen! Someone <u>is playing</u> the violin.
聽！某人正在拉小提琴。

【重點四】有些動詞不能用在現在進行式的句型
裡，以下為常見的，無進行式的動
詞：

1. 感官動詞：hear (聽到)，see (看見)，taste
   (品嚐)，smell (聞起來)，feel (感覺)
2. 心態動詞：agree (同意)，believe
   (相信)，forget (忘記)，know (知道)，
   recognize (認可)，remember (記得)，
   understand (了解)
3. 情緒動詞：desire (渴望)，forgive (原
   諒)，hate (討厭)，hope (希望)，like (喜
   歡)，love (喜愛)，prefer (偏好)，want
   (想要)
4. 表位置的動詞：stand (坐落)，sit (坐落)，
   lie (位於)
5. 表擁有的動詞：belong (屬於)，have
   (有)，own (擁有)

例 I am having a new car. (為錯誤的句子)
→I have a new car. (為正確的句子)

例 He is loving Lisa. (為錯誤的句子)
→He loves Lisa. (為正確的句子)

範例短文 「現在進行式」

Sally and Kevin Are in a Park

    Sally and Kevin are taking a walk in a park. They see many people along the way. Some are walking a dog. Others are jogging. And still others are playing balls. Moreover, there are birds flying in the sky, and there are some ducks swimming on the lake, too. They really enjoy everything that they see in the park.

莎莉和凱文在公園裡

    莎莉和凱文正在公園裡散步。沿路上他們看到很多人。有些人正在遛狗,有些人正在慢跑,還有些人正在打球。此外,天空中有鳥兒正在飛翔;湖面上也有鴨子正在游泳。他們真的很享受在公園裡所看見的每件事物。

【練習題】

I. 連貫式翻譯

1. 操場有很多學生正在運動。
2. 有些學生在打籃球。
3. 有些學生在打棒球。
4. 還有些學生在慢跑。
5. 但有幾個學生只站著聊天。

II. 句子改寫 (請將下列句子的時態改寫為「現在進行式」)

1. Vincent often writes poems at night.
2. They chat with each other on the phone every day.
3. I sometimes go shopping downtown.
4. He studies English every night.
5. Mr. and Mrs. Wang usually take a walk in a park.

III. 請找出（範例短文：Sally and Kevin Are in a Park）一文中有運用到本單元教學討論的「be＋V-ing (現在進行式)」之處，並將該部分劃上底線。

解答

I.

1. There are many students exercising on the playground.
2. Some are playing basketball.
3. Others are playing baseball.
4. And still others are jogging.

5. But some students are just standing and chatting.

II.

1. Vincent is writing poems (now).
2. They are chatting with each other on the phone (now).
3. I am going shopping downtown (now).
4. He is studying English (now).
5. Mr. and Mrs. Wang are taking a walk in a park (now).

III.

1. Sally and Kevin <u>are taking</u> a walk in a park.
2. Some <u>are walking</u> a dog.
3. Others <u>are jogging</u>.
4. And still others <u>are playing</u> balls.
5. Moreover, there <u>are</u> birds <u>flying</u> in the sky, and there <u>are</u> some ducks <u>swimming</u> on the lake, too.

四、現在完成式

【重點一】現在完成式的句型需要用到「過去分詞」(pp)。

★現在完成式肯定句：主詞 + have/has + pp
【某人已經…】

★現在完成式否定句： + not + pp

【某人尚未…】

★現在完成式疑問句：Have/Has + 主詞 +

pp...?

【某人已經…了嗎？】

【重點二】使用時機

1. 某一個動作從過去的某一個時間點開始，一直持續到現在的時間剛好完成。經常和「already (已經)，not...
yet (尚未)，just (剛剛)」連用。

例 The Wang family <u>have</u> just <u>left</u>.
王氏一家人剛離開。

例 My boss is not here. He <u>has gone</u> to Chia-yi.
我老闆不在這裡。他已經去嘉義了。

例 My daughter <u>has</u> just <u>finished</u> her homework.
我女兒剛完成她的家課。

例 We <u>have</u> not <u>paid</u> the bill yet.
我們還沒有付帳單。

例 <u>Have</u> you already <u>drunk</u> the tea?
你已經喝茶了嗎？

2. 指從過去到現在的經驗。經常和「ever
   (曾經)，never(從未)，so far (迄今)，
   once (一次)，twice (兩次)，
   many times (很多次)…」連用。

例 Have you ever seen my husband?
   你曾經見過我先生嗎？

例 I have never been to America.
   我從未去過美國。

例 Kelly has been to Hong Kong many times.
   凱莉去過香港好多次。

例 My brother has visited three countries so
   far.
   我哥哥到目前為止已經去過三個國家。

3. 指某個動作從過去到現在，已經累積多
   少的時間。常和「for + 一段時間」或
   「since + 過去時間／過去式句子」連
   用。

例 I have lived in Taipei for three years.
   我住在台北三年了。

例 Mark has lived in America since 2010.
   從2010年起馬克就住在美國了。

   →〔since (介) 自從〕

例 Bill has worked in Kaohsiung since he got
   married.
   比爾自從結婚就在高雄工作。

   →〔since (副連) 自從〕

範例短文「現在完成式」

Living in Taipei

I have lived in Taipei for three years. And I have visited some famous places since my first year in Taipei. Among them, I like to visit National Chiang Kai-shek Memorial Hall the most. I have been there for more than ten times. Most of the times I go there for a concert by National Chinese Ochestra. And I have been to over six concerts there. However, there are still many places that I haven't visited yet. I have worked in a publishing company since I first went to Taipei. Since then, I have been very busy with my work. That's why I don't have much time to visit many places in Taipei. But I hope I can visit more places when I have free time.

住在台北

　　我已經住在台北三年了。而且從我第一年在台北起，我已經去過一些有名的地方。其中，我最喜歡去的地方就是中正紀念堂。我已經去過那裡超過十次了。大多數的時候我去那裡是為了台灣國樂團的音樂會。而我已經去那裡聽過六次以上的音樂會了。然而，仍然有很多地方我還沒去過。從我最初來台北起，就在一家出版公司工作。從那時起我就忙著工作。那就是為何我沒有很多時間去逛台北的很多地方。但是我希望我有空時可以去更多的地方。

範例短文 「現在完成式」

Shilin Night Market

　　My foreign friend David has never been to Shilin Night Market before, while I have been there many times since I was a little child. David enjoys various snacks whenever he goes to a new country. So I think he would like to try stinky tofu and oyster omelet. I've sent him a message about going to Shilin Night Market together this weekend, but I haven't got his reply yet. However, I don't feel angry because I know he's been busy with work these days.

士林夜市

　　我的外國友人大衛以前沒有去過士林夜市，而我從還是小孩子起，就去過好幾次了。每次大衛去到一個新的國家，他都很喜歡品嚐各種小吃。所以我想他會想嚐嚐臭豆腐和蚵仔煎。我已經傳訊息給他問他要不要這個週末一起去士林夜市，但尚未收到他的回訊。但是我沒有生氣，因為我知道他最近工作很忙。

【練習題】

I. 連貫式翻譯（一）

1. 我學古箏已經二十多年了。
2. 我也已經從藝術學校畢業了。
3. 我從事古箏教學已經三個月。
4. 自從畢業起，我舉行超過五次以上的古箏音樂會。
5. 而且已經和許多學生和古箏演奏家成為朋友。

II. 連貫式翻譯（二）

1. 老師問我：「你學英文多久了呢?」
2. 我回答：「我學英文已經一年了。」
3. 老師接著說：「我原本以為你已經學英文超過三年了。」
4. 然後我問：「為什麼你會以為我已經學英文那麼久了?」
5. 老師回答說：「因為你已經閱讀很多篇超過一千個基本單字的文章了。」

III. 請找出（範例短文：Living in Taipei）一文中有運用到本單元教學討論的「have/has + pp (現在完成式)」之處，並將該部分劃上底線。

IV. 請找出（範例短文：Shilin Night Market）一文中有運用到本單元教學討論的「have/has + pp (現在完成式)」之處，並將該部分劃上底線。

解答：

I.

1. I have studied zither for more than twenty years.
2. I have also graduated from the art school.
3. I have taught zither for three months.
4. Since graduation, I have held zither concerts over five times.
5. And I have made friends with many students and zither musicians.

II.

1. The teacher asked me, "How long have you studied English?"
2. I answered, "I have studied English for one year."
3. The teacher then said, "I initially think you have studied English for more than three years."
4. Then I asked, "Why do you think I have studied English for so long?"
5. The teacher answered, "Because you have read many articles with more than a thousand basic words."

III.

1. I <u>have lived</u> in Taipei for three years.

2. And I <u>have visited</u> some famous places since my first year in Taipei.

3. I <u>have been</u> there for more than ten times.

4. And I <u>have been</u> to over six concerts there.

5. However, there are still many places that I <u>haven't visited</u> yet.

6. I <u>have worked</u> in a publishing company since I first went to Taipei.

7. Since then, I <u>have been</u> very busy with my work.

IV.

1. My foreign friend David <u>has</u> never <u>been</u> to Shilin Night Market before, while I <u>have been</u> there many times since I was a little child.

2. <u>I've sent</u> him a message about going to Shilin Night Market together this weekend, but I <u>haven't got</u> his reply yet.

3. However, I don't feel angry because I know <u>he's been</u> busy with work these days.

五、過去進行式

【重點一】過去進行式的句型需要用到「現在分詞」(V-ing)。

★過去進行式：主詞 + 過去式be動詞 (was/were) + V-ing

【重點二】表示「過去某個時間點」正在進行的動作，要有表示「過去時間點」的時間片語。

例 He was playing the guitar at nine o'clock last night.
他昨晚九點時在彈吉他。

例 They were studying English at ten o'clock this morning.
他們今天早上十點時在讀英文。

【重點三】在過去，若有兩個動作「一短一長」，短的動作發生在長的動作之內，長者用「過去進行式」，短者用「過去簡單式」。

例 He saw her while he was crossing the road.
他在過馬路時看見了她。

【過馬路為長動作，所以用過去進行式 (was crossing)。「看見」為發生在「過馬

路時」的短動作，所以用過去簡單式
(saw)。】

例 When Jane <u>came</u> to see his father, he <u>was</u>
<u>eating</u> his lunch.
當珍來見他的父親時，他正在吃午餐。

【吃午餐為長動作，所以用過去進行式
(was eating)。「來」為發生在「吃午餐」
時的短動作，所以用過去簡單式
(came)。】

【重點四】表示過去同時進行的「兩個長動作」，
兩個動作都用「過去進行式」。

例 While I <u>was preparing</u> lunch, they <u>were</u>
<u>watching</u> TV.
當我正在準備午餐時，他們正看著電視。

例 While Mary <u>was writing</u> a letter, John <u>was</u>
<u>reading</u> a novel.
當瑪莉在寫信時，約翰在讀小說。

範例短文 「過去進行式」

A Family Fight

My family and I had a fight last night. Last night, while Mother was preparing dinner, my two younger sisters and I were watching TV in the living room. Then we were having dinner together when my friend Lisa called me. Lisa wanted me to come to her house soonto help her with the homework. So I went to her house at once without finishing my dinner and washing the dishes. When I came back home, both my sisters blamed me and then we had a fight when someone was knocking at the door. I opened the door and found it was Lisa. Thanks to Lisa's explanation, we finally ended the fight.

家庭爭吵

　　我的家人跟我昨晚發生爭吵。昨晚，正當媽媽準備晚餐時，我的兩個妹妹跟我在客廳裡看電視。然後正當我們一起用晚餐時，我的朋友麗莎打電話給我。麗莎要我快點去她家幫她做家課。因此我馬上去她家而沒有吃完晚餐跟洗碗盤。當我回家時，我的兩個妹妹都責備我，當我們隨後發生爭吵時有人在敲門。我打開門發現是麗莎。多虧了麗莎的解釋，我們終於停止了爭吵。

【練習題】

I. 連貫式翻譯

1. 我昨晚八點時在彈吉他。
2. 那時候我哥在客廳聽音樂，我媽在洗衣服。
3. 然後到了九點時，有人在敲門。
4. 我打開門，發現地上有一個蛋糕和一張卡片。
5. 正當我打開卡片時，大衛來電。
6. 大衛和我哥已經是超過十年的好朋友了。
7. 大衛在電話中告訴我：「這是慶祝你哥哥今天早上贏得比賽的蛋糕。」

8. 當我把蛋糕拿進客廳時，媽媽正在看電視。

9. 而哥哥那時候正在洗澡。

10. 於是我跟媽媽把蛋糕吃了，只留下卡片給哥哥。

II. 請找出（範例短文：**A Family Fight**）一文中有運用到本單元教學討論的「**was/were + V-ing** (過去進行式)」之處，並將該部分劃上底線。

解答

I.

1. I was playing the guitar at eight o'clock last night.

2. At that time, my older brother was listening to music in the living room, and my mother was washing the clothes.

3. Then at nine o'clock, someone was knocking at the door.

4. I opened the door and found there were a cake and a card on the ground.

5. When I was opening the card, David called me.

6. David and my older brother have been good friends for more than ten years.

7. David told me on the phone, "This cake is for celebrating the game that your older brother won this morning."

8. When I took the cake to the living room, Mother was watching TV.

9. And my older brother was taking a bath then.

10. So Mother and I finished off the cake, and only left the card for my older brother.

II.

1. Last night, while Mother <u>was preparing</u> dinner, my two younger sisters and I <u>were watching</u> TV in the living room.

2. Then we <u>were having</u> dinner together when my friend Lisa called me.

3. When I came back home, both my sisters blamed me and then we had a fight when someone <u>was knocking</u> at the door.

六、過去完成式

【重點一】過去完成式的句型需要用到「過去分詞」(pp)。

★ 過去完成式：主詞 + **had** + **pp**【某人已經…】

【重點二】在過去，有兩個動作，一個先發生，一個後發生，先發生的用「過去完成式」(had +pp)，後發生的用「過去簡單式」(V-ed)。

例 The train had left when we reached the station.

我們抵達車站時，火車已經開走了。

【火車先開走後，人才到。所以火車開走用「過去完成式」(had left)，人到用「過去簡單式」(reached)】

例 When they arrived, July had gone home.

當他們抵達時，茱蒂已經回家了。

【July回家後，他們人才到。所以July回家用「過去完成式」(had gone)，他們人到用「過去簡單式」(arrived)】

例 We didn't want to go. We had been to the temple the weekend before.

我們不想去。我們這個周末前就去過那個廟寺了。

【先去過廟寺，所以用「過去完成式」(had been)。之後不想再去，所以用「過去簡單式」(didn't want)】

【重點三】在過去某一特定時間點以前已完成的動作，常用介係詞 by (在…之前)，或是 by the time (到了…的時候) + 句子。

1. 句 (過去完成式) + by + 特定時間.

例 He had finished his homework by yesterday morning.

昨天早上前他就完成了家課。

例 They <u>had left</u> for Tainan <u>by 10 o'clock this morning</u>.
今天早上十點前他們就動身前往台南了。

2. 句 (過去完成式) + **by the time** + 句 (過去式).

例 My boss <u>had left</u> the office <u>by the time you called to me</u>.
你打電話給我時，我們老闆已經離開辦公室了。

例 The bus <u>had left</u> <u>by the time we reached the bus stop</u>.
我們到公車站的時候，公車已經開走了。

範例短文 「過去完成式」

It's Not My Day

    I had an important meeting at two o'clock yesterday afternoon. I had to take a train to attend the meeting. Unluckily, I slept late the day before yesterday, so I got up very late yesterday. When I reached the train station, the train had already left. I had no choice but to take the next train. By the time I got to the meeting room, it was already 3:45 p.m., and the managers that I had to meet had left for their companies. They had finished the meeting by 3:30 p.m.. My boss blamed me badly for the neglect of duty. It was really not my day!

倒楣的一天

　　昨天下午兩點我有一個重要的會議。我必須搭火車去參加那個會議。不幸的是，前天我晚睡，所以昨天起得很晚。當我抵達火車站時，火車已經開走了。不得已我只好搭下一班火車。當我到達會議室時，已經是下午三點四十五了，我必須碰面的經理們都已經離開回他們的公司。他們在三點半前已經開完會。我的老闆嚴厲地責備我怠忽職守。真是倒楣的一天！

【練習題】

I. 連貫式翻譯

1. 昨晚我到社區大學去上英文課。
2. 當我到教室時，老師和同學已經離開教室了。
3. 我打電話問我同學約翰為何教室空無一人。
4. 他告訴我說老師和同學七點十分前就離開前往運動公園參加活動了。
5. 於是我立刻到運動公園去，但是當我抵達時，活動卻已經結束了。

II. 選擇題

1. By the time Vicky got to the restaurant, they _____ their dinner.
   (A) had finished
   (B) finished
   (C) finishing
   (D) have finished

2. He had left for the company when we _____ to his home.
   (A) had come
   (B) come
   (C) came
   (D) coming

3. The boy had finished his homework before he _____ to school.
   (A) goes
   (B) was going

    (C) went

    (D) gone

4. Mary _____ asleep in the classroom by 8:30 this morning.

    (A) falls

    (B) fell

    (C) had fallen

    (D) was falling

5. When the police got to the bank, the robbers _____ away.

    (A) run

    (B) ran

    (C) had run

    (D) running

III. 請找出（範例短文：**It's Not My Day**）一文中有運用到本單元教學討論的「**had + pp (過去完成式)**」之處，並將該部分劃上底線。

解答

I.

1. I went to the community university to take the English class last night.

2. When I got to the classroom, the teacher and the students had already left.

3. I called my classmate John and asked him why the classroom was empty.

4. He told me that the teacher and the students had left for the sports park to join in an activity by 7:10 p.m..

5. So I immediately went to the sports park. But when I got there, the activity had already been over.

II. 1. A 2. C 3. C 4. C 5. C

III.

1. When I reached the train station, the train <u>had</u> already <u>left</u>.

2. By the time I got to the meeting room, it was already 3:45 p.m., and the managers that I had to meet <u>had left</u> for their companies.

3. They <u>had finished</u> the meeting by 3:30 p.m..

七、未來式

【重點一】未來式表達尚未發生的事情，常和表未來的時間副詞連用：**this afternoon** (今天下午)，**tonight** (今天晚上)，**tomorrow** (明天)，**tomorrow morning/afternoon/evening** (明天早上/明天下午/明天晚上)，**next** + 禮拜幾/ **week/month**/季節/**year** (下個禮拜幾/下星期/下個月/明年的…季節/明年)，**the day after tomorrow** (後天)，**in** + 一段時間 (再過…)

1. 未來式肯定句型：主詞 + **will** + 原形動詞

例 He will fly to Hong Kong tomorrow afternoon.
明天下午他要飛去香港。

例 We will go to the movies next week.
下周我們會去看電影。

例 My family will go on a picnic next Sunday.
下周日我們家要去野餐。

例 The manager will have a meeting with us in a few days.
過幾天這位經理將和我們一起開會。

2. 未來式否定句型：主詞 + **will not** + 原形動詞

★ will not可縮寫為won't

例 My boyfriend will not wash the dishes after meal.
我男朋友用餐後不會洗碗。

例 They won't go to the concert the day after tomorrow.
他們後天不會去音樂會。

3. 未來式疑問句型：
(問) **Will** + 主詞 + 原形動詞...?
(肯定簡答) **Yes,** 主詞 + **will.**
(肯定詳答) **Yes,** (主詞 + **will.**) 主詞 + **will** + 原形動詞...

(否定簡答) No, 主詞 + **will not** (或 **won't**).

(否定詳答) No, (主詞 + **will not** (或 **won't**).) 主詞 + **will not** (或 **won't**) + 原形動詞...

例 <u>Will you play</u> basketball with me after school?

放學後你會跟我一起打籃球嗎？

(肯定簡答) Yes, I will. 是的，我會。

(肯定詳答 **1**) Yes, I will play basketball with you after school. 是的，放學後我會跟你一起打籃球。

(肯定詳答 **2**) Yes, I will. I will play basketball with you after school. 是的，我會。放學後我會跟你一起打籃球。

(否定簡答) No, I will not. (或 No, I won't.) 不，我不會。

(否定詳答 **1**) No, I will not play basketball with you after school. (或 No, I won't play basketball with you after school.) 不，放學後我不會跟你一起打籃球。

(否定詳答 **2**) No, I will not. I will not play basketball with you after school. (或 No, I won't. I won't play basketball with you after school.) 不，我不會。放學後我不會跟你一起打籃球。

例 Will your mother cook dinner tonight?

今天晚上你的媽媽會煮晚餐嗎？

(肯定簡答) Yes, she will.　是的，她會。

(肯定詳答1) Yes, she will cook dinner tonight.

是的，今天晚上她會煮晚餐。

(肯定詳答2) Yes, she will. She will cook dinner tonight.

是的，她會。今天晚上她會煮晚餐。

(否定簡答) No, she will not. (或No, she won't.)

不，她不會。

(否定詳答1) No, she will not cook dinner tonight.

(或No, she won't cook dinner tonight.)

不，今天晚上她不會煮晚餐。

(否定詳答 2) No, she will not. She will not cook dinner tonight.

(或No, she won't. She won't cook dinner tonight.)

不，她不會。今天晚上她不會煮晚餐。

【重點二】will 和 be going to 很多時候可通用，但仍有不同之處，如下：

1. **be going to** 有事先計劃的意思，**will** 則沒有經過事先的計劃。

例 He has sold his car because he's <u>going to</u> work in Taipei.
他已經把車子賣了，因為他打算去台北工作。
　　【有事先計劃】

例 My son <u>will be</u> fifteen years old next year.
我兒子明年將十五歲.
　　【沒有事先的計劃】

2. **will** 表「長期或短期」的未來，
be going to 表「即刻的」未來。

例 My husband <u>will come</u> back in three years.
三年後我先生會回來。

例 We <u>are going to play</u> basketball after school.
放學後我們將會去打籃球。

【重點三】「來去動詞」可以用「現在進行式」代替「即將發生的未來式」：

★ 常見的來去動詞：come (來)，go (去)，leave (離開)，start (出發)，arrive (抵達)，return (返回)，depart (離開)，reach (到達)

3
2
4

例 I am leaving for London. 我即將前往倫敦。

例 The bus is reaching Ilan. 公車即將抵達宜蘭。

【重點四】疑問詞開頭的未來式問句

1. (問) 疑問詞 + will + 主詞 + 原形動詞...?
   (答) 主詞 + will + 原形動詞...

例 (問) When will you go to the library?
   你何時要去圖書館？

   (答) I will go to the library tomorrow.
   我明天要去圖書館。

例 (問) When will they hold a party?
   他們何時要舉行派對？

   (答) They will hold a party next Saturday.
   他們下周六要舉行派對。

2. (問) 疑問詞 + be動詞 + 主詞 + going to + 地方名詞／原形動詞...?
   (答) 主詞 + be動詞 + going to + 地方名詞／原形動詞...

例 (問) What are you going to do tonight?
   你今晚要做什麼？

   (答) I am going to practice the guitar.
   我今晚要練習吉他。

例 (問) When is your wife going to school?
   你的太太何時要去學校？

(答) She is going to school at 5:00 this afternoon.

她今天下午五點要去學校。

範例短文 「未來式」

My Dream

I will graduate from the university next month. And I will be nineteen years old then. I have bought many books on job interviews because I am going to work in Taipei. I will leave for Taipei to find a job at the end of next month. Many of my friends wonder what I am going to do after graduation, and I tell them that my dream is to teach in a community university. Since I major in English and have great interest in music, I plan to teach English conversations and English songs and I will also sing every song that I teach my students together with them. I think teaching in a community university is the best way to combine my specialty with interest. I really hope I will make my dream come true.

我的夢想

　　我下個月將從大學畢業。而那時候我將十九歲。我已經買了很多有關工作面試的書，因為我即將去台北工作。下個月底我將前往台北找工作。我的很多朋友對於我畢業後要做什麼感到好奇，我告訴他們我的夢想是在社區大學教書。既然我主修英文，而且對音樂有濃厚的興趣，我打算教英文會話及英文歌曲，而且我會跟我的學生一同歡唱每首教給他們的歌曲。我覺得在社大教書是結合我的專業跟興趣最好的方法。我真的希望我會讓我的夢想成真。

【練習題】

I. 連貫式翻譯

1. 籃球賽今天何時開始?
2. 將在下午三點開始。
3. 你何時要去體育館呢?
4. 我快要出門吃午餐了。
5. 吃完午餐後，我將直接去體育館看球賽。

II. 將下列句子加入 **will** 改寫為未來式
1. I go to the movies. (tomorrow)
2. Kelly goes to church. (next week)
3. There is a baseball game at the stadium. (tonight)
4. My parents go to the sports park. (after work)
5. The president comes here. (the day after tomorrow)

III. 請找出（範例短文：**My Dream**）一文中有運用到本單元教學討論的「**will + V**」或「**be going to +V**」之處，並將該部分劃上底線。

解答

I.
1. When will the basketball game start today?
2. It will start at three o'clock this afternoon.
3. When will you go to the gym?
4. I am going out for lunch.
5. After lunch, I will directly go the the gym to watch the game.

II.
1. I will go to the movies tomorrow.
2. Kelly will go to church next week.
3. There will be a baseball game at the stadium tonight.

4. My parents will go to the sports park after work.

5. The president will come here the day after tomorrow.

III.

1. I <u>will graduate</u> from the university next month.

2. And I <u>will be</u> nineteen years old then.

3. I have bought many books on job interviews because I <u>am going to work</u> in Taipei.

4. I <u>will leave</u> for Taipei to find a job at the end of next month.

5. Many of my friends wonder what I <u>am going to do</u> after graduation, and I tell them that my dream is to teach in a community university.

6. Since I major in English and have great interest in music, I plan to teach English conversations and English songs and I <u>will</u> also <u>sing</u> every song that I teach my students together with them.

7. I really hope I <u>will make</u> my dream come true.

八、被動式

★被動式的句型需要用到過去分詞 (pp)。

【重點一】簡單式被動

1. 現在簡單式被動：
   主詞 + be動詞 (am/is/are) + pp + (by + 受詞)

例 The door is opened by Sally. 門被莎莉打開。

例 The book is written by Vicky. 這書是維琪所寫的。

2. 過去簡單式被動：
   主詞 + was/were + pp + (by + 受詞)

例 The building was built by us in 2013. 這棟大樓是我們在2013年所建造的。

例 The cars were washed by my father. 這些車是我爸爸所清洗的。

【重點二】進行式被動：進行式與被動式的結合

1. 現在進行式被動：
   主詞 + be動詞 (am/is/are) + being + pp + (by + 受詞)

例 At present a new park is being built in this community.
   目前一座新公園正在這個社區建蓋中。

例 The sich child is being checked by a doctor.
這個生病的小孩正由醫生檢查中。

2. 過去進行式被動：
主詞 + **was/were** + **being** + **pp** + **(by** + 受詞)

例 I was being blamed by my mother when you called me last night.
你昨晚打電話給我的時候，我正被我的媽媽責罵中。

例 The window was being opened by a thief when we got home this afternoon.
今天下午我們到家時，窗戶正被一個小偷打開中。

【重點三】未來簡單式被動: 未來式與被動式的
結合

★主詞 + **will** + **be** + **pp** + **(by** + 受詞)

例 Your class will be taught by Miss Ho next spring.
明年春天你們班將由何老師所教導。

例 The gift will be bought by her boyfriend tomorrow.
禮物明天將由她的男朋友所購買。

【重點四】完成式被動：完成式與被動式的結合

1. 現在完成式被動：
主詞 + **have/has** + **been** + **pp** + **(by** + 受詞)

例 The gas has been checked by your father.
   瓦斯已經被你的父親檢查過了。

例 The rooms have been cleaned by me.
   這些房間已經被我打掃過了。

2. 過去完成式被動：
   主詞 + **had** + **been** + **pp** + (**by** + 受詞)

例 The letter had been delivered by the
   postman when I reached the post office.
   當我到達郵局的時候，信已經被郵差送走
   了。

例 The cake had been eaten by the students
   when the teacher came to the classroom.
   當老師來到教室時，蛋糕已經被學生們吃
   掉了。

【重點五】有助動詞的被動式

   ★主詞 + 助動詞 + **be** + **pp** + (**by** + 受
   詞)

   〔常見的助動詞：**should, can, might,**
   may, must〕

例 More training should be offered by my
   company.
   更多訓練應由我們公司所提供。

例 The window may be broken by a thief.
   這個窗戶也許是被小偷所打破的。

例 The work <u>can be finished by</u> Mr. Chen.
　 這工作可由陳先生完成。

例 The floor <u>must be cleaned by</u> Mary.
　 地板一定是瑪莉所打掃的。

【重點六】無被動語態的動詞：英文有些動詞無
　　　　　被動語態，常見的如下：

1. 感覺類動詞：
   look (看起來)╱ **sound** (聽起來)╱ **smell**
   (聞起來)╱ **taste** (嚐起來)╱ **feel** (感覺起
   來)╱ **seem** (似乎)

例 The cake tastes good.
　 這蛋糕好吃。（為正確的句子）
　 The cake is tasted good. (為不正確的句子)

例 This idea sounds good.
　 這主意聽起來不錯。（為正確的句子）
　 This idea is sounded good. (為不正確的
　 句子)

2. 事實類動詞：
   happen (發生)╱ **occur** (發生)╱ **take place**
   (舉行)╱ **break out** (爆發)╱ **belong to** (屬
   於)╱ **exist** (存在)╱ **consist of** (包含)╱
   arrive (抵達)

例 The game will take place next Friday.
比賽將在下周五舉行。（為正確的句子）

The game will be taken place next Friday.
(為不正確的句子)

例 The watch belongs to me.
這隻錶是我的。（為正確的句子）

The watch is belonged to me.
(為不正確的句子)

範例短文 「被動式」

Score

I am often blamed for low score on the test. I try to study hard, but may be disturbed by many things. My classmates often ask me to play basketball with them. And my good friends usually invite me to join in their activities. I know I will be punished by some of my strict teachers if I don't get a good grade, but I just can't resist the temptation to be with my classmates and friends and have a good time with them. Although I have been blamed or punished for low score many times, I still cherish friendship more than score.

分數

　　我常常因為考試低分而被責罵。我嘗試用功，但也許會被很多事情干擾。我的同學常常要我跟他們一起打籃球。而且我的好朋友經常邀請我加入他們的活動。我知道如果我沒有拿好成績，我會被一些嚴格的老師所處罰，但我就是無法抵抗想跟同學及朋友在一起度過美好時光的誘惑。雖然我已經因為低分被責備及處罰很多次了，我還是珍惜友誼多於分數。

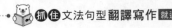

範例短文 「被動式」

An Unforgettable Taxi Ride

One evening, finding bus after bus filled with people, Lily decided to go home by taxi. She was so exhausted that she dozed off shortly after she got into a taxi. About fifteen minutes later, the taxi reached her house. She was roused from her light sleep when the taxi stopped. As she tried to pay the fare to the taxi driver, she found that her purse had been left in the office. What's worse, when she tried to open the front door of her home to get some money, it occurred to her that her keys had been put in her purse. It was indeed an unforgettable taxi ride. However, she hopes a similar experience will never happen to her again.

搭計程車的難忘經驗

　　有一天傍晚，由於發現每一班公車都擠滿了人，莉莉決定搭計程車回家。她很疲倦，所以在進入計程車不久之後就打瞌睡了。大約十五分鐘之後，計程車抵達她家。當車停下來時她從瞌睡中醒來。當她試著拿車費給計程車司機時，她發現錢包遺留在辦公室了。更糟的是，當她試著打開她家的前門去拿點錢，她想起來她的鑰匙放在錢包裡了。那次乘坐計程車的經驗真是令她難忘。但她希望將來不會再遭遇類似的事情。

【練習題】

I. 連貫式翻譯

1. 我昨天過馬路時被機車撞了。
2. 接著我馬上被送去鄰近的醫院。
3. 在我到達醫院之前，撞我的騎士已經先到了醫院。
4. 他跟我道歉，還說已經受到我家人的責備。
5. 還說新的衣物已經放在我病房的床上了，也會替我付醫藥費。

II. 將下列句子改寫為被動式

1. I have finished the homework.
2. My mother grows these flowers.
3. She will clean the room.
4. Mr. Chen invited her to dinner.
5. The construction workers are building the bridge.

III. 請找出（範例短文：**Score**）一文中有運用到本單元教學討論的各種時態的「被動式」之處，並將該部分劃上底線。

IV. 請找出（範例短文－**An Unforgettable Taxi Ride**）一文中有運用到本單元教學討論的各種時態的「被動式」之處，並將該部分劃上底線。

解答

I.

1. I was hit by a motorcycle when I was crossing the road.
2. Then I was immediately taken to a nearby hospital.
3. Before I got to the hospital, the motorcyclist that hit me had reached there.
4. He apologized to me and said that he had been blamed by my family.
5. He also said that new clothes had been put on the bed in my ward, and he would pay the medical fee for me.

II.

1. The homework has been finished by me.
2. These flowers are grown by my mother.
3. The room will be cleaned by her.
4. She was invited to dinner by Mr. Chen.
5. The bridge is being built by the construction workers.

III.

1. I am often blamed for low score on the test.
2. I try to study hard, but may be disturbed by many things.
3. I know I will be punished by some of my strict teachers if I don't get a good grade, but I just can't resist the temptation to be with my classmates and friends and have a good time with them.
4. Although I have been blamed or punished for low score many times, I still cherish friendship more than score.

IV.

1. She was roused from her light sleep when the taxi stopped.
2. As she tried to pay the fare to the taxi driver, she found that her purse had been left in the office.
3. What's worse, when she tried to open the front door of her home to get some money, it occurred to her that her keys had been put in her purse.

永續圖書
線上購物網

www.foreverbooks.com.tw

◆ 加入會員即享活動及會員折扣。

◆ 每月均有優惠活動，期期不同。

◆ 新加入會員三天內訂購書籍不限本數金額，

　即贈送精選書籍一本。（依網站標示為主）

專業圖書發行、書局經銷、圖書出版

永續圖書總代理：
五觀藝術出版社、培育文化、棋茵出版社、犬拓文化、讚
品文化、雅典文化、知音人文化、手藝家出版社、璞申文
化、智學堂文化、語言鳥文化

活動期內，永續圖書將保留變更或終止該活動之權利及最終決定權。

抓住文法句型，翻譯寫作就通了

雅致風靡 典藏文化

親愛的顧客您好，感謝您購買這本書。即日起，填寫讀者回函卡寄回至本公司，我們每月將抽出一百名回函讀者，寄出精美禮物並享有生日當月購書優惠！想知道更多更即時的消息，歡迎加入 "永續圖書粉絲團"

您也可以選擇傳真、掃描或用本公司準備的免郵回函寄回，謝謝。

傳真電話：（02）8647-3660　　　　電子信箱：yungjiuh@ms45.hinet.net

姓名：		性別： □男 □女
出生日期： 年 月 日	電話：	
學歷：	職業：	
E-mail：		
地址：□□□		
從何處購買此書：		購買金額： 元
購買本書動機：□封面 □書名 □排版 □內容 □作者 □偶然衝動		
你對本書的意見： 內容：□滿意□尚可□待改進　編輯：□滿意□尚可□待改進 封面：□滿意□尚可□待改進　定價：□滿意□尚可□待改進		
其他建議：